The Lev

From the desk of
Author
Cherisse M Havlicek

Dear Debbie
And the Love
Continues!
Cherisse
xx
2022

The Lewis Legacy

The Lewis Legacy

A Present / Past SAGA

by

Cherisse M Havlicek

Once again, I must thank the Good Lord for leading me down this path. His guidance led me to the towns of EL Dorado and Lawrence, Kansas. He has given me this passion that has been my light in the darkness.

I must thank my family, again and still. They have never told me to stop telling them my ideas or reading them passages for the umpteenth time! Thank you, Allan, Arthur, Alisse Havlicek and my mother Doris Basile. You have all given me support even if it was with reverse psychology

Again, I must thank all my pre-publication readers. Their thoughts, ideas, suggestions and support have made me continue with this process when it all seemed overwhelming.

Finally, I must thank the Lawrence Visitors center. I went there to get general information on the area and was immediately pulled into the history of the Massacre that was on display. I knew I wanted to do a sequel to my ANNA AT LAST novel but seeing this historically important event from the past put lots of ideas into my head and I knew that I had to include it in my next book. Thank you, Susie N., who was working there at the time, you patiently answered my questions and gave me your personal information in case I had any more.

ISBN-13: 978-1-7326799-2-4

DEDICATION

This book needs to be dedicated to the real survivors of the Quantrill Massacre of 1863, the townspeople of Lawrence, Kansas. Though, I have used poetic license to create this story from the facts presented, it was a real and horrific event that left Lawrence in ashes and with over two hundred unarmed souls dead. They were fathers, brothers, sons, businessmen, farmers, preachers and everything in between. The loss of these men left hundreds of children without fathers, women without husbands and ransacked burnt businesses without owners to rebuild. The townspeople left to bury and carry on were the real heroes. They survived and thrived despite the hardships. I hope that I have been able to do them justice with this tale.

***

This novel, is a work of fiction. The 1863 Massacre actually took place. I have taken my imaginary characters and interspersed them with the names of real people affected as to give life to this account. It is done to entertain and hopefully enlighten my audience to an important event in history. The characters and events in the 1937 story are all the work of my imagination. Any resemblance to actual persons, living or dead or actual events is purely coincidental.

ONE

Monday, September 27th, 1937
in Lawrence, Kansas

Anna is holding the baby and looking at her, and says. "You have my heart, little one."

"I thought your heart belonged to Henry. Are you fickle, Anna?" Without looking up, Anna loses her smile. This is the voice that haunts her nightmares – *John Walker's voice!* She can feel her heart pounding in her ears. She is not facing him, so he cannot see the look on her face. She knows that her fear must NOT show. "Anna, did you hear me?" She puts a forced smile on her face. Then the thought crosses her mind, *our plan worked, he is here.*

She says without turning, "Shush, the baby is asleep." She puts her child in the basket and puts the basket on the bed. She says to the little one, "There, safe and sound." She turns to face him. When she does, she has her little derringer in her hand. She was going to ask him how he got past the security but . . . she wakes up!

Henry is out of the bed, already and she can smell the coffee brewing on the stove. She sits up and shivers and puts her hand over her swollenness. "Oh, little one, we have to stop having these dreams!" She puts on her robe and slippers and paddles off to get a hug from her husband. His hugs always take the nightmares away. She knows it was another one about John Walker but thankfully, the details are becoming blurry with the daylight.

****

Anna just finishes cleaning up the Colonel's lunch dishes in the 'diner-style' kitchen of the Main House. She is moving a little slower these days due her 'bun in the oven' as her Henry likes to say.

She is seven months along and all seems well. She did not get this far in her first pregnancy. In the year that she did not know her identity, Anna miscarried at about five months along. She was still in so much pain from the attack. Two years ago, she was kidnapped, raped, beaten and run down by a truck. She was in a coma for months and afterward was very frail and thin. She suspected that she might be pregnant but . . . she dreaded the thought that it was her attacker's baby so she refused to think about it.

Then, at five month, along, when the Colonel roamed the house around the clock, Anna was up all day and night with him. The Colonel, in his seventies, is very confused. The official diagnosis is dementia. He sleeps on and off all day and talks to his dear departed wife and cannot remember that his grandchildren are grown-ups.

So, between her frail condition and trying to keep up with the Colonel, her baby was not to be. After she lost her little girl, she lost her will to live. The Colonel would sit at her bedside for hours and tell her of his Julia, and his two beautiful grandchildren that he raised after their son and his wife were killed. He and Julia were childhood sweethearts, she moved away and he joined the Cavalry in 1877, and they lost track of each other. When the Colonel was engaged to a woman near the Fort in Leavenworth, he wrote to Julia to ask her a favor and they didn't stop writing to each other. After only a few letters he asked Julia to marry then wrote to the woman in Leavenworth to break-up. They married immediately after seeing each other for the first time in years 'And Lived Happily Ever After.' The Colonel always says.

That story felt so familiar to her. She felt that it was her story, too. She had a feeling that someone was out there loving her and missing her. She would hear his low silky voice in her dreams but his face was always elusive. At that time, all her memories were elusive.

After Anna's attack and abandonment, Carolyn's dog and car companion, Rocco, sniffed her out on the drought stricken land on Legacy Plantation. Anna was naked and barely alive with her shoulders broken, her nose broken, her neck fractured, and a swollen brain from the direct impact with the headlamp of her father's Ford truck. In the Hospital, Carolyn thought to call her Rosanne instead of Jane Doe and she stayed Rosanne for almost a year. Until it was discovered that she was Anna Rose Masters from EL Dorado, Kansas.

EL Dorado is only 137 miles away but it was as good as 1000 miles because the attacker said he drove for only about an hour before he raped and killed her in a barren field. He was so sure that he killed her that he convinced everyone she was dead - except her Henry. He spent the whole year going sixty miles in all directions looking for her. He could not let himself believe that she was dead, even with John Walker's confession.

Anna's thoughts of those days were interrupted by the Colonel ringing the bell for her in the sitting room. She went through the formal dining room to get to where the Colonel was in his chair with a blanket over him. "Did you need something, Colonel?" She asked.

"Rosanne, could you start a fire for me? I am chilled to the bone. I don't remember such a cool September, do you?" He was shivering.

"Colonel, I will get Henry to start it for you. I am not allowed to carry the wood, right now." She said as she put her hand on her swollen belly. She doesn't correct him for using the name that Carolyn gave her instead of her real name. She knew that since he met her as Rosanne, she will be Rosanne to him, forever. "He is working near the sunflower fields, I think. I will ring the bell to bring him to the house. After I ring for him, why don't I take you to the bathroom? Okay? Moving around will warm you up anyway."

She left the sitting room and went back to the kitchen to exit out the back door to ring the giant bell, just off the veranda. The sun was shining brightly but there was a crispness to the air. She rang three times then paused a moment and rang three more times. She looked at her watch and waited two minutes to do it again. As soon as she stopped with the second round she heard his truck horn repeat the signal.

Since learning of her pregnancy, Henry refused to leave the property of the Main house, just in case she needed him. He went downtown and ordered this 'Liberty Bell' style bell that was three feet in diameter where the clang hits. It makes such a loud noise, that it can be heard anywhere on the 10 acres surrounding the

Main house. They had a signal in place to let him know why she was ringing. Three clangs, pause, three clangs meant that she needed him for manual labor. Two clangs, pause, two clangs, pause, two clangs meant that a meal was ready. Five clangs, pause, five clangs meant come right away. Non-stop clangs meant an emergency. She is so lucky to have him be so thoughtful and concerned enough to devise this system.

Henry drove up in his Da's old truck to the back door. He exited the vehicle and came to her. He took his hat off his head and bowed down and said, "You rang, milady? How may I be of service?" He straightened up, when their eyes met, they both smiled. Her brown hair's red highlights were reflecting the sun and her wavy hair was cascading down to her shoulders. "You look lovely this afternoon, my dear. Is that a new waistline you have on?"

His eyes dropped to her swollen belly and she followed his gaze. Her hands went instinctively to cover her girth. "Oh, Henry, you are really something. What am I going to do with you?" She holds out her arms as he simultaneously moves into them.

"The answer is always the same, my dear. Whatever you want to do with me." They briefly kiss, before he pulls away. "Now, what did you need me to do?"

She reluctantly, pulls away too and says, "The Colonel would like a fire and we have no wood in the sitting room." She turns to enter the house. "Where were you when I rang? Did I stop you from doing anything important?"

"I was walking the sunflower field, checking the heads. They are close to ready but some have bug damage. After I start Colonel's fire, I will call Joshua and see what he would like me to do. He is very smart about these kinds of problems. Carolyn did a great job running this place but Joshua's education has proven very beneficial." They walk to the sitting room. "Afternoon, Colonel. Did you want a fire? I will get the wood, right away." Henry bends down and checks the fire grate and the flue. "I have always loved this fireplace and room. It's your favorite spot, too, I see." He winks at the Colonel.

"Henry, I am shivering, can you hurry?" He looks

up pleadingly.

Anna goes to his side. "Come on Colonel, while Henry gets the wood and starts the fire, why don't I take you to the facilities?" She bends down to help him move his blanket out of the way so he can stand. She instinctively puts her arm under his left armpit and does the count, "One, two, three, up." She supports him as he straightens up to walk.

"Rosanne, I think you need to stop getting me up. You might hurt the baby. Henry was right here, why didn't you let him do it? Julia said that I shouldn't let you lift me anymore. She is very worried about you. Didn't she tell you that herself, this morning?" He says as she walks him to the bathroom.

"No, Colonel, Mrs. Julia doesn't talk to me, like she talks to you. But you can thank her for me, please and I will try to remember to let Henry help you. Do you want help in the bathroom?" He is sometimes lucid then shy and he is sometimes confused and has no reservations about her toileting him.

"No, Julia says that I must do it on my own, without your help. She will get mad at me if I do not listen." He enters the room and softly closes the door.

Anna stands at the door and waits. She loves this sweet caring man who was a strapping figure on his horse when he was in the Cavalry in the late 1870's. Now he is very thin and shrunken.

His Julia, though gone for twelve years now, is very insightful and is always giving him the proper advice. It still gives her the chills when he talks about talking to her and repeats what Julia tells him. Anna feels like she knows Julia from all the conversations that the Colonel has had with her these last two years.

Last year, when he had kidney stones and almost died, he became violent and delusional with the pain he was experiencing. He pushed her away so hard that she fell and reinjured her neck. They were both sent to the hospital and after a few days, they allowed Anna to visit him in his room. She was in a wheelchair and a neck brace and the Colonel, went on and on about Julia being very mad at him for hurting her. He said he did not remember doing it, but was very sorry if he did, because he loved her and would not want her hurt for anything. He was near tears. Anna told him not to worry that she did not blame him for the accident. Now why and how could he not remember hurting her but think Julia was mad at him for hurting her? After that, Anna never told the Colonel that Julia was gone or dead. She believed that his Julia was very real, if only for his eyes or only in his mind.

She heard the toilet flush and the sink turn on for him to wash his hands. Moments later, he opened the door, and was surprised to see Anna waiting for him.

"I'd like to go back to my chair, now, Rosanne. Can you start a fire and make me some hot tea? I am chilled to the bone." He already forgot about Henry.

Anna ignored the slip and said, "Henry is working on the fire, Colonel and I will go put the kettle on for some tea. Then I need to start our super Supper Celebration." She returns him to the sitting room and goes straight to the kitchen to make his tea. She then goes to start the prep work for this evenings meal.

Even when she did not remember that she was Anna, she knew how to cook. She worked in an EL Dorado diner for a short while and got in the habit of cutting up all the veggies and getting out all the ingredients, way before starting the actual cooking.

Now that Joshua has graduated from college and is running the farm, Carolyn has taken to getting patents for her water irrigation inventions and has set herself up in her own business. She had put this off during Joshua's time at college. Carolyn, is three years older than her little brother and, also is a graduate of Washburn University in Topeka. She has an Engineering degree and thought of some pretty ingenious ways to combat the drought. Many farm owners were after her to sell them the system she designed, but they all had to wait.

So, every meal is a full house now. Anna, Henry and his Da, eat at the Main house with the Colonel, Joshua, and Carolyn, every night except Saturday and Sunday; which are technically Anna and Henry's days off. Anna loves to cook large Sunday dinners, though, and has her parents and / or siblings come up at least once a month to supper, from EL Dorado.

Tonight, is a special night. Henry wanted to take her

out to dinner to celebrate but she insisted that she make a meal with her whole family present. The six of them will be driving up from EL Dorado, and they will be spending the night here at the Main house, courtesy of Carolyn and Joshua.

Two years ago, today, Henry asked Anna to be his wife. One year ago, today, they were married in the Front parlor of this house. They spent that whole engagement year not knowing if the other was out there alive or looking for them. Anna was attacked the morning after Henry proposed and was given her identity back just two days before they decided to call the Preacher to the house and make them man and wife. Anna can recall how unwilling Carolyn was to make that 'ridiculous' (Carolyn's words) call to Pastor Jonas. All of Anna's friends and family were present for an 'Anna's Alive Party' so why not have them all be witnesses to the nuptials, was Anna's thinking, that day. Once she knew she was Anna, she knew she did not need to wait another day to wed the man that spoke to her in her dreams - Henry.

Anna is getting very excited to see her parents, Judd and Judy, as well as her younger siblings, Melinda and Mathew and their spouses Mark and Susan. It has been a few weeks since they were altogether. She cannot wait for her mother to see how big the baby in her is getting. The child is very active now, and her mother has not had the privilege of feeling it kick yet. This will be the first grandchild on both sides.

The kettle takes to singing, bringing her out of her happy daydreams and she finishes up the Colonel's hot tea and brings it to him in the sitting room. He is dosing, again, in front of the now roaring fire. She gently puts her hand on his shoulder to wake him. "Colonel, the tea is hot, as is the fire. I will be in the kitchen, if you need me. I have lots of work to do for tonight's dinner."

A woman's voice behind her said, "I told you that I would be happy to take everyone out to dinner to celebrate. You should not go through all this trouble in your condition."

Anna turns to see Carolyn. She is just a little shorter than her but her no-nonsense bearing makes her appear taller, for some reason. "Carolyn, you know cooking for me is not trouble. It brings me such pleasure to feed my loved ones, and you know this." She walks over to her and gives her a kiss on the cheek. "But thank you for the offer. You are always too good to me."

"Nonsense, I am just the right amount of good to you. How is the Colonel, today? Any problems?" She says to them both.

"I have been on my best behavior, Carolyn. I promised your grandmother that I would not let Rosanne help me get up or anything else that could harm her."

Carolyn shrugs off the comment about her grandmother and says, "Good Colonel, we all need to help Anna be careful, don't we?" She kisses her grandfather on the cheek and turns to Anna. "Is Henry in the house? I need to show him something."

"What do you need, Carolyn? I just got off the phone with Joshua at the Farm Office. We have a slight insect problem with the sunflower crop." Henry says from behind them in the sitting room doorway.

"That is related to what I want to show you. It is a new thing I cooked up to spray away the insects. Come out to my car, it's a little heavy for me to carry." They both go out the front door and Anna goes back into the kitchen to get working on dinner.

A few hours later, they are all done with the delicious meal served in the dining room. The men go into the sitting room for cigars.

Professor Edward James, Carolyn's beau, has come down from Topeka to join the celebration. It was the Professor's class investigation of Anna's case that led to solving the mystery of her missing identity.

The women clean up the dining room in no time, and talk a mile a minute the whole time they are doing the dishes. Of course, Carolyn, Melinda, Susan and Judy, don't let Anna clean a thing.

Once they are finished, they call the men in the Front parlor so they can all be together. They each brought a little gift for the Happy Couple's Day. It was a wonderful evening that came to an end, all too soon. Everyone started yawning and stretching very dramatically, saying that they had a hard day of work and that long drive has left them exhausted.

Henry's Da said that he and Judd were going to stay up late and talk, (they were childhood friends) and that Da will most likely spend the night on the couch in the sitting room, so not to disturb them by coming in too late.

Henry smiles at Anna and whispers, "I think they are trying to give us a little alone time." Anna blushes bright red.

"Well, let's not waste the opportunity!" She whispers back to him. She stands up and kisses them good-by and with a "See ya in the morning!" They were out the door.

Anna and Henry live in the first home that the Colonel built for his Julia. As the Colonel's farm and property grew, so did the homes that he built from scratch. The Main House being the crowning jewel. Anna's place was very modest. It had two bedrooms, indoor plumbing, a dining room, a living room, and a small eat-in kitchen. The best part of the perfect floor plan was that the bedrooms were on opposite sides of the home. Henry has always taken care of his father, Da. Now Da will not hear them making love at night, which Henry warned her could happen to her embarrassment.

Anna gets on the porch and to the door before Henry does. He calls to her, "Anna, my love, wait for me."

She turns to him. He is smiling, which makes her smile in return. He is such a handsome man, she thinks, with his Roman nose, grey eyes and wavy black hair that he always struggles to keep out of his eyes. "But, Henry, I would love to get started with our celebration . . ." She trails off.

He is next to her, now. "I just wanted to carry you over the threshold, like I did last year." He bends down to gently pick her up. "I was so worried about doing this with your injured neck, remember?" He steps through the doorway with her. "But now I am carrying two of you. It's a good thing I keep fit, little mama." He kisses her while she is still in his arms. "My whole world is in my arms, right now. I love you so much, Anna." His lips are on hers again.

"Well, fit or not, you do not need to hold up the whole world this long. I don't want you to use up all your energy, this early. I have plans for the rest of our evening, together. Now put me down, husband dear."

He puts her down. "Anna, you asked Dr. Mason if we can still be together, that way, didn't you? I do not want to harm the baby or hurt you."

"Oh, Henry, we will be just fine. Trust me." She winks at him. These were the very words she used on their wedding night with him. He was so worried about causing her neck pain or making her relive her rape. She reached up to push the stray strands of hair out of his eyes. "You do trust me, don't you?" He just smiled, then blushed at the possibilities.

TWO

Tuesday, September 28th, 1937
In Lawrence, Kansas

Anna and Henry are awake at first light, despite their late night. She fell asleep in her favorite position, in his arms. She was so lucky to have found Henry, not just once but twice. Like the Colonel and his Julia, Anna and Henry were childhood best friends. Both of their fathers lost their farms between the plummeting wheat prices, the depression and the long drought. They were separated for four years before running into each other while roaming the harvest at a tomato farm in EL Dorado.

Their fathers were friends from childhood and had arranged the marriage of Anna and Henry, before they had any time to get reacquainted. It was decided that the engagement would not be official until Henry formally asks her to marry, which took a few very complicated weeks. He fought the notion of settling down, and he felt that he had outgrown Anna and was more interested in her outgoing, little sister, Melinda. He learned the hard way that he could not have been more wrong. Anna was the only one for him . . . before, now and forever! He can honestly say; he loves her more with every passing day.

Anna was in a hurry to get to the Main house to make breakfast for her family. She knew that her mother would take over the duties if she did not get there. The Masters had stayed a few months in the off season with the Lewis family to be with Anna. It had been a long year of missing her and thinking she was dead, so now they wanted to make up for lost time.

But EL Dorado had it draw on the Masters, too. Her father, Judd, had been given a management job at the Johnsons Family Farms and felt very loyal to Grant Johnson. Also, there were the two weddings. Melinda and Mark married before the Holidays and Matthew and Susan married in the early spring. Susan loves to tell everyone that she married Matthew just to be Mark's sister-in-law a second time. Mark's first wife who died

13

during childbirth was Susan's older sister.

By the time Anna and Henry get to the Main house, Judy Masters has, indeed, made breakfast for everyone present. Anna rushes in and is trying to apologize for being late.

Her baby brother says, "We are surprised to see you at all, this morning, sis. Did you let Henry get any sleep last night?"

"Matthew!!" cried Anna, Judy Masters and his wife, Susan, at the same time. "How could you say such a thing?" Blushed his young wife. She just turned 19 and is older than her 18-year-old husband.

Judy Masters walked behind Matthew and gave him a small swat on the head. "We did not raise you to be crude, young man. Married or not! Now apologize to your sister."

Before he could say anything, Henry said, "I am glad you asked about my welfare, Matthew. Yes, Anna let me get a few winks last night." Anna turns to him horrified but she relaxes when he winks at her. And I am getting a few winks in now." They all laugh.

Carolyn changes the subject. "What does everyone have planned today? Anything interesting?"

Joshua speaks up, "Henry and I are going to try out your new sprayer on our sunflower heads. Care to come see your invention in action?" Before Carolyn can answer, Judd says, "I'd love to come along. I am fascinated by what you've come up with, to help us all farm better.

Just then, a bell is heard from upstairs. Anna starts to leave her breakfast plate when Joshua jumps up. "Stay with your family, Anna, I will get the Colonel up and dressed and down here." As he turns away, he winks at Carolyn. Anna knows they are part and parcel of this 'Anna watch' conspiracy.

"I am perfectly fine doing my duties. The baby and I are very healthy, according to Dr. Mason. You do not have to baby me, honestly."

Henry reaches out to grab her hand and give it a squeeze. "Just enjoy it, Anna, we are all doing it because we love you." Everyone in the kitchen nods in agreement.

Melinda speaks up for the first time. "Anna, why

don't we women do a little baby shopping. I am sure you need to get some things. Diapers, bottles, a baby carriage, I think you are close enough now, not to jinx yourself."

Susan looks puzzled so Judy explains, "We have a superstition about buying something for the unborn before being six months along. Anna is seven months, now, so she is safe."

"Oh, I see. And I wanted to get something for my little one-to-be, today. I guess I must wait a few months, now. Darn it!" She smiles as she waits for everyone to put it together that she is pregnant.

Matthew's jaw drops. "Do you mean you are . . .? We are . . .? A baby, really? I thought we agreed to wait until after I get out of college before we started?" He says with a happy grin on his face.

"Well, um . . . surprise! God had something else in mind. Are you happy, Matthew?" He goes to her and lifts her chin up and kisses her sweetly on the lips. Matthew is six foot four inches and Susan is just about five feet. So, it's a good thing she was seating in one of the stools. He did not have to bend down, as far.

"I am very happy, Susan, I wasn't the one who wanted to wait. Are you happy?" He looks at her with all seriousness.

"Young man, can't you see me smiling? And I thought you were a quick study!" She kids him. She like to joke about being older than him whenever she can get it in. "I was seriously excited about shopping for baby things, though. Must I wait four whole months before I buy, anything?" She looks around.

"YES!" The Masters girls all say at once with great enthusiasm. Then, they laugh as they see Susan pout.

"Don't pout, Susan." Says Matthew hugging her, "The time will fly in no time. I promise."

Judd had crossed the room to Susan. "I would love to congratulate the soon-to-be parents!" He opens wide his arms and he takes in both his son and his bride. Then it is a free for all as they all hug and kiss them.

Carolyn interrupts, "Does that rule count for getting something borrowed? I think we have an old chest upstairs that might have some baby stuff in it. Joshua found an old key ring in the Farm office that might unlock it. It has been locked in an attic, my whole life and I am dying to see what is in it. Anyone up for an adventure?" All the young women nod.

Judy says, "Why don't you, young ones, go do that, I will feed the Colonel and clean up here." Anna goes to object but Judy puts a hand up to silence her. "I will go home right now if you give me a hard time, here Anna, I swear I will." She says with all seriousness. She looks around the room at all the stunned faces the smiles. "Boy, no one can take a joke around here, anymore."

An hour later, Carolyn, Anna, Melinda and Susan have each taken a turn on their knees at the old dusty trunk in the attic. They brought the key ring that Joshua has found as well as every other skeleton key that they knew of in the house. Carolyn tried them all and nothing fit, so Anna took them from her and started over. Still nothing fit. "Who's trunk is this, do you know?" Anna asks.

"I asked my Grandmother Julia when I was a child. We were living in one of the other houses at the time. She said it was her mother-in-law Elizabeth Lewis' trunk. It sure looks old enough. It is very heavy, also, so it's filled with something from my family's past. I haven't thought about this trunk in years, until Joshua brought home this huge ring of keys. I am really disappointed that nothing will open it."

Melinda is now giving it a go with all the keys. "If we cannot open it with a key, did you want to bust it open? Or should we go shopping, instead?" She asks Carolyn as she is working up a sweat, with the keys.

"Well, it has been up here a long time, it will wait a little longer. Let's hit the stores."

There was a loud cry from the corner of the attic from Susan. "Come look at this treasure!" Susan held up a large white wicker basket, she found from under some old blankets. It was two feet long and a foot wide. "This is the perfect Baby bassinette, don't you think? The little one can sleep the night in it as well as travel. It's beautiful. Can Anna borrow it? And when her babe outgrows it, can I borrow it?" Susan asks, so excited.

Carolyn looks at it. "I remember Joshua in this. Yes, of course, Anna can use it." Susan pouts. "You can also, Susan." They all went down to the main level with smiles on their faces at their find.

THREE

Thursday, September 30th, 1937
In Lawrence, Kansas

Things are a little back to normal, now that Anna's family are all back in EL Dorado. Henry, his Da and the Lewis's are still being very protective of Anna and are commandeering her duties. After lunch, today, Carolyn told Anna to take the rest of the afternoon off. Her feet were swelling and she looked very tired. So, Henry brought Anna home and made her nap. After she slept, her feet looked back to normal size. She made a small supper for the three of them. Henry and Da did the dishes, while Anna read.

But Anna was restless. She wanted to organize the baby things that she and her family bought on Tuesday afternoon. All the things came home with Anna late in the evening after her whole family left for EL Dorado. Anna always gets a little glum when her family leaves so she kept busy at the Main house and forgot all about the stuff in the baby basket in her bedroom. She went into the bedroom and unpacked the items onto her bed.

She had all sorts of goodies for the little one. Lots of cloth diapers, little shirts and booties. Baby bottles, dishes, spoons, comb and brush set, baby blankets and, of course, the beautiful bassinette.

"Henry, are you busy?" She calls him into the bedroom. As he stands in the doorway, she says, "I'd like to keep the baby in our room for the first year but he or she will need her own room, eventually. Do you think we can put walls up in the dining room and make it a small bedroom? I doubt Da will want to share his room with a baby so we will need to do something, don't you think?"

He shrugs his shoulders. "I can change the dining room to a bedroom easily, I guess. We will be a little cramped in here, in the meantime." He looks around the 12-foot square room with no closets. They have clothes hanging in 2 wardrobe cabinets and have 2 dressers. "If we move the 2nd wardrobe to that wall and move our bed against that wall. We could use this dresser for the baby basket and as dressing table.

She is nodding her head as he is talking. "Can we move it, now?" She gets up from the side of the bed and walks to the wardrobe. She opens one of the drawers at the bottom and bends down to use the frame to pull.

Henry gets red, "What do you think you are doing, Anna? You are so stubborn. You cannot move furniture at seven months pregnant!" He tried to push it himself but did not move easily. "Let me call Da." He sticks his head out the doorway. "Da? Could you give us a hand?"

Frank comes in and after Henry explains their plan, he takes Anna's side and puts his hands in the drawer frame. They walk/lift the six-foot wardrobe to the new spot on the other wall. Frank pushes it against the wall. When he removes his hand from the frame, he knocks something off inside and it clatters down. "What was that, you think?" He opens the next drawer down from the one he was holding and sees a skeleton key laying on Anna's sweaters. "Was this yours?" He turns to Anna and holds up the key.

"No, it isn't. We do not have anything here with that kind of key. I wonder what it fits?" She has another thought. "I wonder if it will open that trunk in the attic at the Main house. I cannot wait to try it tomorrow." She looks at the open spot along the way where the wardrobe was, "I think we can get another little dresser here, we need one just for the baby's things." She says as she points to the stuff on the bed. "There were more dressers in the attic. Maybe you can bring one down for me, Henry?" She gives him large eyes and bats her eyelashes as if flirting.

"Anna, don't make cow eyes at me, I'd do anything for you." Henry chuckles.

"And if he wouldn't, I would." Says Frank.

Henry and his father are cut from the same cloth. Same tall frame, same long face and Roman nose. Same wide smile. Same loving kind personality. Same joking nature. It was easy living with these two. Anna felt herself blessed and walked to Da and gave him a kiss on the cheek, then walked to Henry and gave him a kiss on the lips. "I am very lucky to have you both, taking care of me." She picks up the baby bottles and other food related items and heads to the kitchen to find a cabinet to put them.

When she gets back to the bedroom, Frank and Henry were in a serious conversation and stopped suddenly when she walked into the room. "Okay, you two, what are you both up to?" She looked at Henry, while Frank quickly leaves the room. "We said no secrets, Henry, remember?"

He shakes his head, not wanting to say what he needs say. "Come sit on the bed, Anna. We have bad news from EL Dorado."

She sits on the edge of the bed. He holds her hands and sits next to her on the edge. "Matthew called me at the Farm office. He said that John Walker was arraigned and released, yesterday, pending the new trial. I immediately called the District Attorney, he said that the trial will begin on Monday. We will drive down on Sunday night. We can stay at either Matthew's or Melinda's. You will only be needed the one day, or two days. Unless you want to stay for the whole thing. It is a shame that they cannot retry him on the attempted murder. They said it would be double jeopardy, because he was already tried for murder. The D.A. said since they did NOT try him for abduction, assault or rape, those charges should get him back in jail."

"I don't know which I am more afraid of, his being free or testifying against him. Will he be in the courtroom to see me?" Henry nods. "Oh dear, I do not think I will sleep a wink until after Monday?" She shakes her head then covers her face with her hands. "Henry, how am I going to look at him and still talk?"

"Anna, darling, look at me." She takes her head out of her hands and looks at him. "No, I mean during the trial, just look at me. Have eyes for me only! Talk calmly, clearly and slowly. You have told me the story as it has slowly come back to you. We will work on it so that you can tell what you remember from beginning to the end, without leaving anything out or getting too upset to talk about it. It happened a long time ago and talking about it cannot hurt you anymore." He has taken her hands in his and raises them to his lips and kisses them. "I will not let anything hurt you, anymore."

She pulls one hand away and pushes a long wavy lock away from his eyes and tucks it behind his ear. Then she runs her hand along the side of his face. "I do not know what I would do without you, you know?" She kisses him lightly on the lips, then looks in his eyes. She loves his smoky grey eyes! "Henry, promise me it will be alright. I will believe it, if you say so."

"Anna, I do promise, no matter what happens at the trial, it will be alright. You have me and our little one-to-be and nothing is more important than our family. Memories or the telling of a horrible story from a long time ago will not hurt us. I promise. Now let's find a place for this baby stuff for tonight and tomorrow we will go explore the furniture in the attic of the main house. I know Carolyn is dying to know what is in that trunk after all these years."

FOUR

Friday, October 1st, 1937
In Lawrence, Kansas

Anna and Henry were at the Main house at their usual time, seven a.m. Anna starting the baking, which she prefers to do in the morning. Twice a week, she bakes bread loaves and twice a week she makes cookies and pies. Once a week, she bakes cakes and treats for Rocco, the German Shepard that insisted that Carolyn stop her truck so he could go to help Anna, who was lying naked and near death.

Carolyn had come down for breakfast and was thrilled when Anna told her about finding the skeleton key. "Oh, let's go right up and try it." Anna shook her head, no. "Too many things in ovens." Then her hand caresses her belly. "I am not referring to the babe this time." They laugh. "I am afraid I will go up to look for a dresser and lose track of time. If you can wait about 45 minutes, I should be free by then." The Colonel's bell started ringing from upstairs. "I am being summoned, anyway. Finish your breakfast Carolyn." Anna goes to get the Colonel washed, dressed and ready to come down the stairs. This is a little early for him, but she might as well take advantage of it. She heads up the stairs.

Joshua meets her at the Colonel's door. "How are you feeling, this morning, Anna?" He reaches for the door knob. "I got this, I am sure you have something in the oven that needs attending to."

"Joshua, are you trying to take my job away?" She reaches out and removes his hand. "The Colonel is my responsibility. Don't you have a Plantation to run or something?"

"Anna, did I ever tell you that you are adorable when you are being obstinate?" He smiles at her. "The Colonel is my grandfather so that trumps your responsibility. Now go bake something." He now takes her hand off the knob.

The bell started ringing again, from behind the door and Henry's deep voice cuts the tension between them.

"I think Joshua should help the Colonel, Anna. And I agree with him, you are adorable when you are obstinate. I came up here to give you a hand but since Joshua is here . . ." Henry says with a little hint of annoyance in his tone.

The smile on Joshua's face disappears at the presence of Henry. Anna shrugs her shoulders. "I give up, I am outnumbered." She smiles at Joshua. "What do you want for breakfast, I will have it ready when you get downstairs?"

"Whatever the Colonel is having." He turns the doorknob. "Good-morning, Colonel. I am here to get you dressed. Anna will start your breakfast. What would you like this morning?"

The Colonel thought for just a moment. "Hot tea, two slices of toast and cookies, please. Good morning, all. Joshua, I really need to make water, can you get me to the bathroom, quickly?" Joshua has his arm around the tall frail man and leads him to his private bathroom.

Anna and Henry head back downstairs. Once on the lower level, Henry turns to Anna. "I don't like him saying you are cute. That's my job. I know he had designs on you, while you were Rosanne, and it makes me nervous."

Anna stops suddenly. She starts laughing. "Henry, that is the funniest thing, I think I have ever heard you say. I love Joshua like a brother. Even when I did not remember you, it was always only you. I always told him that you were out there and that he should forget about me. Yes, Joshua wanted more, but he has never crossed any line that you need to worry about. I promise." She reaches up and puts her arms around his neck. "I love thee to the depth, and breadth and height my soul can reach." She kisses him lightly on the cheek then their lips meet softly at first, then they get lost in a moment of passion as if there are alone in the world and this is the only moment that has ever existed.

Anna breaks away, slightly. "Henry, do you want to . . . um . . . find a spot where we could be alone?"

Henry holds her at arms distance. "Anna, are you suggesting we take a nap with breakfast barely under our belt? What's come over you? You are almost insatiable, lately. Not that I am complaining, but I could get fired 'boinking' the help in the middle of the day, you know. Besides, you have cakes in the oven, and once I got started with you, they'd be burned to a crisp!"

Anna laughs, "Boinking the help? I like that word, you made that up, didn't you? I do have two more breakfasts to get ready. Be my guilty pleasure later, okay?" She gives him another kiss on the cheek. "I better get the kettle on for tea." She heads back into the kitchen.

Once back in the kitchen, Carolyn says, "How is the Colonel, this morning? Are your cakes almost done? I want to go into the attic, with this key!"

Anna fills the kettle with hot water and puts it on the stove. Then she gets the four slices of bread and puts them in the two toasters. She goes to the cookie jar and plates about eight homemade cookies. Then she peeks in her oven. "The Colonel seems very lucid this morning. He has not had a bad day in a while, now that his kidneys are behaving. Cakes need another minute or so. By the time I do these dishes, the cakes will come out and we can go try out the key."

Joshua brings the Colonel in and Carolyn goes to her grandfather and gives him a kiss on the cheek, good morning. "Did you sleep well, Colonel?"

"I don't remember." He says with a smile. This is his little joke. He is always making fun of himself or uses his dementia as a ploy to disobey the rules. His little dog, Robbie is very happy to see him and the Colonel bend down to pick him up. Robbie starts licking his face, so happy to be in his arms. "Okay, good boy, enough of that." He puts the wiggling dog back down.

Anna finishes the dishes and has their tea and toast ready to feed Joshua and the Colonel. Then she takes her cakes out of the oven.

"Finally!! Let's get upstairs. Do their dishes later, will you? Come on, I know this key will work!" Carolyn sounds like an excited schoolgirl instead of a twenty-four-year-old.

It is easy for Anna to always catch Carolyn's excitement. She owes so much to this wonderful woman. She found her on the property and called her doctor to pick her up and she paid for all her medical expenses. Then she brought her home to live with them. Anna and the Colonel hit it off so well, that she slowly took over the Colonel's daily care. Carolyn and Joshua did not stop trying to find her real identity. They hired private detectives to no avail. Joshua called Professor James for a referral and instead the Professor suggested having his Senior class take over the investigation.

Then a colleague in EL Dorado wanted to share the investigation. That Professor turned out to be the retired Sheriff that arrested John Walker and took him to 'find' Anna's body for a reduced sentence. When Professor James filled in the details known about the girl they called Rosanne; the retired Sheriff said he solved the case.

Anna feels that she owes this family, everything. "Come on, sister, let's go on an adventure."

They head up to the attic and Carolyn is on her knees in an instant, with the key in the trunk. She gave it a couple of twists and the lock made a noise. A snap and a click later and the latch was undone. Carolyn giggles with excitement and looks at Anna, "Are you ready?" She lifts the trunk lid.

The trunk was filled to the brim. There were clothes, journals and papers. On top of everything was a homemade Oval Sampler that read: *'The Lewis Legacy* with the year *1866* and the initials *EPL.* Hanging from the main oval were seven smaller ovals each with a name on it. The names were: *Ian, Joseph, Lizbet, William, Marjorie, Carolyn* and *Charles.* Carolyn squeals, "Ooohh, this is my Great Grandmother Elizabeth's trunk. She made grandfather an identical sampler that had his name hanging and one for his Julia. This is one of the reason's the Colonel calls the farm Legacy Plantation. These names are all my aunts and uncles. I want to hang this in our parlor! What a find!"

Anna looks through some of the books. "These are her journals, it seems. There are so many."

Carolyn looks at them. "We should get them in order and read them to the Colonel. He would love hearing his mother's thoughts and words. She died long before I was born. There must be 40 books in here. If the stories she tells are any good, we could get them published. She would have been alive during the Civil War, so they have historical value."

Anna is taking the books out and looking at the dates inside them. "This might take a while to sort out. Let's stack them by year at least." They begin doing that. The journals weren't put in the trunk in any sort of order, it seems. As they get deeper into the trunk, Carolyn takes over the bending into the trunk and handing them to Anna after she locates a date. They get lost in the work, for over an hour.

"Anna, Carolyn, are you both still up there?" Henry calls up to them from the base of the staircase. "Are you ladies doing alright?"

Anna goes to the top of the staircase and says, "We've got the trunk open and it contains Carolyn's grandmother's journals. We are organizing them to read in order. I haven't looked around for a dresser, yet. Do you want to come up here and look with me?"

Henry bounds up the steps. "I thought you'd never ask. I did not want to intrude on your girl adventure, though." He kisses her cheek when he gets to the top step. "Wow! That is a lot of books." He saw the Sampler and picked it up. "Are these all of Colonel's siblings? I did not know he had that many. Are any of them still alive or in the area?" He asks Carolyn.

"All but my Uncle Ian. He died while he was in his twenties, I think. Then the farm went to Grandfather. The rest are spread out here and there. You know, the Colonel's birthday is at the end of the month, I should surprise him and see if I can get all his siblings together. He'd be just thrilled."

Anna and Carolyn continue organizing the journals while Henry looks around for a dresser. What he finds instead is a highchair. "Look Anna, a highchair! This is a nice one, too. No little dresser, though. We'll need to buy one, I think." He brings the highchair closer to the stairwell. "We don't need to bring this downstairs just yet. Babies stay on mother's milk for six months or more, don't they?"

"I don't know." Both Carolyn and Anna answer at the same time. They all laugh.

"This baby is in for a real treat, if none of us even

knows how long before they eat solid food!!" Anna quips. "Maybe I should get some baby books."

"Or maybe, Great Gram Beth, will tell us. She had seven little ones." Carolyn says as she is paging through one book. "I think we are done and I think I have the first journal here. The first entry is dated today, October 1st in 1866. This is the one we will read tonight after supper, then."

FIVE

October 1ˢᵗ, 1866. Monday
An Excerpt from the Journal of Elizabeth Lewis
In Lawrence, Kansas

My husband, William, has been so thoughtful as to make a present of this journal. Of course, he says it's for his own sanity for I am always leaving scribbled-on sheets of paper or parchment about. I've wanted to tell the story of how we survived THE QUANTRILL MASSACRE in 1863 on Lawrence, Kansas and how we didn't. We were more fortunate than some. Our home was untouched, but we did have our losses, too. Some days, the losses weighed very heavily upon me, but I had my children and I had to be strong for them. Young Willie was only four years old, Lizbet (Lizzie) was ten, Joseph was twelve and Ian, the oldest, was fourteen. They were way too young to have lived through these things, let alone to have made a difference, in our outcome. There was no rhyme or reason as to who survived that horrible time. With four hundred and fifty men who washed over Mt. Oread like a giant wave to rob, kill and burn, it was a miracle any of us survived, at all.

My name is Elizabeth Lewis. I knew William Quantrill from his first time in Lawrence back in 1859 or '60. He went by the name of Charlie Hart, at that time. I was a laundress just before the war. I owned Elizabeth's Laundry. I had six women who worked for me, at that time. They were all wizards with a washboard. Nathan Stone's City Hotel was my biggest client. Every morning, his servants would come down to my shop with bags of laundry. Nathan's patrons were usually in a hurry to get their clothing back as quick as can be. We had to be careful not to mix up the contents of the bags. Each bag belongs to a different room and no one wanted Mrs. Hawkins in Room Ten to get Mr. Butler's starched shirts from Room Twelve. Nor would Room Twelve want Mrs. Hawkins underpinnings.

Anyway, Charlie Hart was a frequent guest in Room Eight. He was very fastidious about his clothing. He would come to our shop to give us specific instructions as to how to clean his things. At the time, though, we thought that very odd, since we all heard rumors of his rough escapades. He liked to spend his day at the Ferry Landing giving a hard time to newcomers who were against slavery and who talked of abolition. He hated free-soilers, but Lawrence and all of Kansas, at that time was slave-free. Charlie had his hands full robbing these new free-soil arrivals, while trying not to get caught.

I had young Willie with me at the laundry. He was just a few months old then and still at the breast, so I could not get too far away for long. In fact, all my children were at the laundry with me, before and /or after school. Charlie was very nice to my children. He was a schoolteacher back in Ohio. Charlie was in his early twenties and very, very smart, but he never talked down to the little ones. He would hold Young Willie for long stretches at a time. He would help Lizzie with her hair bows and say that she reminded him of his sister who was a seamstress back in Ohio. He would buy Joseph and Ian penny candy from the Sweet Shop and help them with their lessons. Charlie seemed the fondest of little Lizzie for he would play Tea with her, often. I know that Charlie's soft spot for my little ones, was the reason I survived. I could not believe that this good natured mild man named Charlie Hart, who read story books aloud to amuse my young ones would become the mastermind of the largest, most vicious civilian massacre of the Civil War!

One time, my husband had come in town from our small farm to get supplies and have lunch with us. Charlie Hart was visiting and insisted that he take us all to the Eldridge Hotel for lunch as his guests. William was suspicious of his motives but he got to know Charlie. Charlie was about 5'10" but he had a thin frame. He had sandy brown hair and a small pencil thin mustache on his pox scarred face. He had an easy air about him and soon William considered him a friend.

Our Sheriff Walker, though, thought very differently of Charlie. After getting multiple complaints from the newcomers, the District Attorney Joseph Riggs put out a warrant for his arrest. The charges ranged from kidnapping, horse thievery, burglary, larceny, to arson. It was thought that he also stole slaves out of Missouri and then sold them back to their owners for the reward. He and a man named Jack Herd were even suspected of killing three Quakers from Missouri because they were abolitionists. No charges were ever filed for that crime, though. Once the warrant went out for his arrest, Charlie stopped visiting Lawrence and Lawrence became the town that he had to get even with.

Before that though, on one morning back in 1860, Charlie came rushing into Elizabeth's Laundry. He was very frazzled and said that he misplaced his mother's diamond ring. He thought it was in one of his shirt pockets. After a thorough search of his bag of laundry, he did not find it.

Weeks later, when he was in town, again, I asked him if he found his mother's ring. He did not know what I was talking about, until I reminded him that he was looking in his shirt pockets for it. He laughed and said that he gave the ring to Lydia Stone, Nathan's fourteen-year-old daughter, as thank you, for nursing him back from a near fatal illness. He said he was too much into his cups at the time, so he did not remember it the next day. He said that Nathan was upset with him for giving his daughter a ring without his permission. Charlie apologized. He said that the ring had no strings attached and that Lydia can keep it without worry that he would expect any favors from her. He told me that he said to Nathan that he respected him and his daughter and would not abase her in any way. Nathan let Lydia keep the ring.

Poor Lydia would be sorry later. Nathan was killed during the Raid over that ring.

SIX

Saturday, October 2nd, 1937
In Lawrence, Kansas

On Saturdays and Sundays, Anna and Henry are off, though Anna still likes to make Sunday dinner. Normally, they try to sleep in, then have a light breakfast at home. Maybe run a few errands in town. This Saturday is not normal. Henry wants Anna to practice her testimony for the trial.

"Henry, I am shaking already. I do not know if I can do this. What if I can't? Does that mean he will be free to roam the streets again?" Anna and he are sitting across the kitchen table with coffees still in hand.

"I think the evidence will speak for itself. You must put things in order. Now, start at the beginning. Date, time, place."

"Saturday, September 28th, 1935. 7:30 in the morning. I was driving into town to start my shift at the diner. It was the morning after you proposed . . ." She finishes the tale and sighs deeply then puts her head in her hands.

Henry reaches for her face and takes it from her hands. He was proud of her for getting through the story for the first time without stopping. He knows she needs to go over this again, but it cuts through his heart hearing what she endured because of him. He is the one that punched John Walker at that game on Thursday. If only the coward tried to get even with him in person, instead of hurting his Anna. As crazed as John was with hate at the time. The deepest wound that John could give him was making him lose the love of his life. "Anna, I am so sorry for you having gone through this because of me. I hate that you must relive it. Are you okay?" He paused and though it hurts him as much as it hurts her, he asks. "Do you want to go over it again?"

After she retold the story two more times, they start to pack for their trip. They won't leave until after service tomorrow. They will be staying at Mark and Melinda's. This way Anna with have the comfort of her Ma, beside his own support.

Anna wants to make a big meal for the Lewis family tonight. She feels bad for having to leave the care of the Colonel for a few days. After they are packed they head over to start the meal prep.

They stay after dinner and Carolyn reads two entries in Elizabeth's Journal.

SEVEN

October 2nd, 1866. Tuesday
An Excerpt from the Journal of Elizabeth Lewis
In Lawrence, Kansas

I cannot believe how much I wrote last night after putting the little ones to bed. This is my time. William knows that I need an hour or two in the evenings to read or write without being disturbed. He calls it 'Beth Time'. He even made a little rhyme to kid me about it. He says, "First it is Bath Time, then it's Bed Time and finally it's Beth Time which make us all Happy because a Happy wife means a Happy Life!" He is so good to me. I married a good man.

Now back to my tale. The Lawrence Massacre took only four-hours but it was four long hours of horror. It started just before dawn on August 21, 1863. William Quantrill had long stopped using the Charlie Hart name. He was a Rebel Guerilla Leader of the most cunning kind. He was known for his calm in the most dangerous situations and his take NO prisoners attitude. It was more than an attitude, Quantrill ordered his men to never take prisoners and never leave wounded foes on the field. For years, he raged war against civilians and Federal troops for the South's cause before the Confederacy was even formed. He and his army fired many a shot before the first shot fired at Fort Sumter, the official beginning of the war.

We had heard that in 1862 he was officially mustered into the Confederate Army as a Ranger Company Captain. He had several soon-to-be infamous raiders whetting their appetite for blood and lawlessness, such as the James-Younger gang of brothers and Kit Dalton with them. Jesse and Frank James were cousins to Cole Younger and they were all teenagers cutting their teeth on the exploits of their leaders.

We also heard, later, that he went to Richmond to request a commission of Colonel for all the battles he fought and won for the South. He was denied, by the Secretary of War, himself, but Quantrill came back and lied to his men that he earned the rank of Colonel. That amount of hubris was the beginning of the end for Lawrence.

The Colonel started to lose his hold on his men while he was on his way home from Richmond until a very unfortunate accident, just a week before the Lawrence Massacre. The Union Major General in charge of the Missouri / Kansas border had rounded up fourteen female sympathizers of the Bushwhackers (pro-slavery ruffians). Some were the relatives of Quantrill's chieftain Bill Anderson, and the Younger brothers. The building that held them collapsed in on itself. My husband, William, was new to the Brigadier General's Regiment and told me that armed guards were also killed in there but Quantrill said it that it was all on purpose. He had everyone convinced that it was an execution. Bloody Bill Anderson lost one sister and had another one crippled by the rubble. My family paid dearly for Bloody Bill's loss.

This collapse catastrophe worked out to Quantrill's advantage. He had to prove to the powers at Richmond that he was no longer the petty thief and ne'er-do-well Charlie Hart but that he was a military mastermind. That is why Quantrill never fired a shot in Lawrence. William Quantrill came into town dressed in a Sunday Best suit (of course he had 4 Navy Colts in his belt) but was fresh shaved and even had on toilet water, while his four hundred and fifty men were unwashed, unkempt, unrested, unshaven, and soon to be drunk on alcohol, power and the blood-letting.

At the end of the ordeal, almost 200 unarmed men and boys, lay dead or dying. My kin were among them.

My William was not in town during the Massacre. Thank God. He would have been killed just for being in his Union blues. He had joined the Cavalry, just a few months earlier. He was in 'A' Company of the Eleventh Kansas Cavalry. They were up in Fort Leavenworth under Brigadier General Thomas Ewing Jr.'s Command. My William was with the General when a courier was sent from a Colonel Pike who watched Quantrill's men march past him unmolested near the Missouri state line. (Pike claimed that he had too many men out on patrol so he would have been severely outnumbered.) William asked the Brig. General to send a telegram to Lawrence to warn them but Ewing was not convinced that the town was in danger. My William asked for leave to go to Pike's regiment and find out which way the men were going and possibly catch up with them, to find out their destination. He was denied that also. Ewing did send out his own couriers to varies towns that might get attacked but none of them were Lawrence. Lawrence seemed too well protected, too far away from the Missouri border and too large of a town to be in danger. But they did not know that it was William Quantrill who led army. If they had known, my William would have had no trouble convincing Ewing that Lawrence was the town that he hated the most. Our town made Charlie Hart feel like a nothing. So now, Quantrill wanted to make the town of Lawrence 'nothing'. His orders were to kill every man and boy old enough to hold a gun, and then burn the down the town!

My older boys, Ian and Joseph, were in the Fourteenth Kansas Regiment which was just boys playing soldier. They were quartered in a tent camp on the East side of Massachusetts Street. They were in Union blues and were being taught to march but were never instructed on or given any weapons or ammunition. All those poor boys, sound asleep at five a.m., in those tents! It's been three years and my hand is shaking trying to tell what happened to all those poor boys. With the Enemy charging at full gallop and screaming a Rebel yell, they were shooting into the tents just prior to trampling through them. My poor boys were never more afraid. Joseph still has nightmares. Ian's best friends were killed in front of them. One rider grabbed a running boy by the hair and dragged him fifteen feet before letting go of him then shooting him in the back of the head. My boys were on the far end of the camp and were woken by the sounds of guns and the screaming of their friends. They ran under a porch of a nearby house.

Unfortunately, that gave them a perfect view of the carnage. Ian's friend, John Watson, was shot and crying for help just a dozen or so feet away from my boy's hiding place. Ian said he was going to get John and drag him under the porch with them. Joseph pleaded with him to stay hidden but Ian could not allow someone who needed help go unaided. (Oh, he is so much like his father!) He looked around before crawling out then ran to his friend. John kept calling his name, calling attention to Ian. Ian tried to quiet him but a bullet did it for him, instead. Ian was pulling him toward the porch when John's head exploded from a bullet hitting it. Ian froze in place. Joseph saw the whole thing, and was yelling to him to come back to the hiding place. Suddenly, a trail of bullets hit the dirt near Ian's feet and the porch where Joseph was hiding. Ian watched them go toward his brother and that was enough to get him moving. A few bullets hit the porch, some even went through the wood planks. Ian started running for the porch and the bullets flying left the porch and started their way back toward Ian. Ian zig zagged, then threw himself the under the porch just in time for a bullet to hit him. Joseph helped pull him in and when he looked up there was a Raider bending down and looking under the porch for them. They scooted as far back as they could and in the dim light of daybreak were not seen. Or if they were seen, the Raider decided to spare them. He could have just fired blindly at that angle and would have killed them both, but didn't. Ian was in terrible pain from his bleeding leg wound but my boys stayed silent under that porch for hours. By the time the sound of gun fire in the town stopped, Ian was no longer conscious and Joseph had to make his way out and get help for his brother.

Joseph first went to Elizabeth's Laundry, thinking that I or some of my women would be there to help him. The laundry was in ashes. Most of the stores in the business district were in ashes, including my uncle's Gun Shop which was a small store at the end of the business district. Joseph then went to the City Hotel. He knew that Nathan Stone's brother lived there and that he was a Doctor. Joseph entered the Hotel, from the rear and saw Lydia Stone hiding in the kitchen pantry. She called him to her and put her hand over his mouth to shush him.

There was a ruckus in the front of the Hotel. It was one of the Raiders. Quantrill and his Army had left the town and his Sacred Protection of Lydia, Nathan and the Hotel left with him. One of the last Raiders left, Larkin Skaggs, wanted that ring on Lydia's finger. He had taken it, earlier that morning but Lydia told Quantrill and he made Skaggs return it. Skaggs was now very drunk and feeling invincible and didn't give a hoot, that Quantrill had given his friends his protection. A diamond ring is a diamond ring, after all. He ordered everyone out of the Hotel. He shot several of the men that surrendered. Then he shot several times blindly into the Hotel. Nathan himself went outside to remind Skaggs that Quantrill was a friend. He barely got the words out, when Skaggs shot him dead with a bullet in the stomach. Skaggs never got down from his horse. He swayed a bit from the drink then rode out of town, in the wrong direction. On his way, back through, fifteen-year-old Billy Speer (the Newspaper publisher's son) shot him with his mother's rifle. Then an Indian named White Turkey walked up and shot him with an arrow in the heart. Later, the Skaggs body was dragged by his horse up and down Massachusetts Avenue by the free Negros in town, because earlier Skaggs had dragged our Union Flag in the same fashion.

But I am off the subject, so my Joseph was at the Hotel but Nathan and his brother the Doctor are now dead. Lydia (just sixteen years old, then) is beside herself with grief. He runs back out to the street and finds his way back to Ian, under the porch. He drags him out and begins to carry him down the street. Now Ian is two years older than Joseph and built with a larger bone structure (like his dad and grand-dad Clyde) so he was a few pounds heavier but my (tall but thin) Joseph was determined to get him help. People were all out in the streets now. They were either trying to put out fires or trying to give medical attention to those in need. Ian needed it badly.

Major Preston Plumb, Ewing's Chief of Staff had just ridden in with thirty troops. It was their dust cloud that Quantrill's lookouts saw on Mt. Oread, that ended the massacre. My William was one of the thirty that rode hard for eight hours to get to Lawrence. Joseph had been carrying his brother for about 15 minutes when his father found him. Ian lost his leg that day but thank God, not his life.

EIGHT

October 3ʳᵈ, 1866. Wednesday
An Excerpt from Elizabeth Lewis's Journal
In Lawrence, Kansas

I do not know why I am dragging this event up again. I've wanted to put it all down on paper from the beginning, but I was too raw from the loss. All my friends and relatives are still raw from it all. So many deaths and so much destruction! They said that the property damage amounted to well over a million dollars. I can barely imagine an amount that size! The loss of life and innocence was too great to calculate. After I finished writing late last night, I cried myself to sleep. My William heard my sobs and held me in his arms and reminded me that we are now safe. The War is over and Quantrill is dead. Life goes on.

It sure does. I have had two babies since the Massacre and am with child once more. It is odd that we thought that I was barren when we were first married. It took 3 years before Ian came. I am married 20 years now and I am getting with child faster than ever before. I blame that on the Massacre also. When I start to brood over the past and my sweet William comforts me, one thing leads to another, and well, a blessing comes from my sorrow. So now I have Ian (seventeen), Joseph (fifteen), Lizbet / Lizzie (thirteen), young William (seven), Marjorie (two), and Carolyn (one). So, three boys and three girls, this babe will be a tie breaker. I do think seven children is quite enough. I am getting too old to deliver them safely and have them come out perfect. Also, we are stretched quite thin on the farm income. I didn't try to salvage my laundry business because I would have had to rebuild the whole shop in the midst of my sorrow and I could not.

I lost my business, my Father, my Uncle and my newborn baby girl during the Massacre. My oldest child lay losing his leg and almost his life and he needed me at his side and I failed him just as I failed my Father.

Before the War, on William's family Farm, his father

Clyde, my father Charles and my Uncle Daniel all lived with us to help work the land. My Uncle also was a gunsmith and owned a very small store downtown, just a block down from my 'Elizabeth's Laundry House'. My father was unwell; his mind was leaving him. He was to the point of needing someone to dress him and help him with eating etc. He was in his late fifties but his mind was just off somewhere. He roamed around the cabin at night, took too many daytime naps and was very opinionated when awake. Uncle Daniel had become his primary caretaker, since I had the babies and the Laundry business.

We live a few miles southwest of town but we heard the shooting as soon as it started. We knew it was trouble since Mayor George Washington Collamore forbade guns in town. The town had a large practiced Militia but the guns were stored at the armory. In hindsight, that is why the Massacre so easy to accomplish. Quantrill split his four hundred and fifty men into forty-five units and each of the units had its own mission. Charlie, I mean Quantrill had a specific Death List. Abolitionists, Preachers, law-makers and many others were on it to complete his Revenge.

With my William, away in the Cavalry, my Uncle and Father-in-law Clyde wanted to see what the shooting was about and help if they could. They took our only rifles and left on their horses, leaving me with my father and the two young ones. Father heard the shooting, also, and was very worried about the older boys. He was making sense to me but he was acting like a caged animal, insisting on being allowed go find Ian and Joseph.

Young Willie always could tell when Father was upset and began pacing with him. Little Lizzie was helping me with breakfast. I assumed that my boys, father-in-law and uncle would return in a short while, with a large story to tell and a large appetite to go with it. As I was frying the meat, Father said that he and Young Willie would feed the chickens and collect eggs. At almost four years old, collecting eggs was Young Willie's job so I appreciated Father taking him to the barn. When they did not come back directly, I went to the door and found only the full egg basket. Father and Young Willie were gone! I grabbed Little Lizzie and went to the barn to see if the Buckboard was still there. It was but Father's Kentucky mare was missing. He must have taken Willie to find Ian and Joseph. I did not know what to do. I guess that I will put Nellie to the buckboard and go look for Father and Willie as they look for Ian and Joseph. Did I mention that I was with child and the time for my confinement was near? I manage to get Nellie hitched, Lizzie climbed into the buckboard and I struggled to climb in myself.

As I made my way to downtown, I could see the columns of smoke rising from the business district. My laundry shop was in that area. What could be happening? We rode hard, and my priorities wavered. I had to see what was becoming of my business on my way to the far side of town where my boys were encamped. It was past the time for my friends to arrive to work. Were they in harm's way? I was now getting very anxious for my family and my future. I needed to work to make ends meet until harvest time.

As I pulled up to the front of my shop, I had to put my handkerchief over my mouth because the smoke was thick in the street. Lizzie started screaming. On her side of the buckboard sat a bushwhacker on his horse looking at her, as mean and unhappy as a man could look.

I stood up in the carriage. "Leave her alone!" I shouted at him. He looked me up and down and his eyes rested on my swollenness. He blushed and looked me in the eye, then tilted his head and said, "Sorry Ma-am, I didn't mean to scare you or the little lady, here." He pulled on the reins to turn his horse around.

"Wait! What is going on here? Why are you doing this?" I yelled to him.

"William Quantrill's orders, Ma-am." Was all he would say as he kicked his horse into motion.

I gasped. Charlie Hart was behind all this? I thought and said, "Wait! Where is he? I need to talk with him. He knows me. He knows my kids and they are out here in danger. Can you take me to him?"

"No Ma-am. I have my orders. I can tell you that he has commandeered and set up command at the Eldridge Hotel. You might be able to see him there." With that and a final kick to his horse's flanks and he *was galloping away.*

NINE

Sunday, October 3rd, 1937
In EL Dorado, Kansas

Henry drives to Mark and Melinda's place in EL Dorado in the early afternoon. Anna is so happy to be in the kitchen with her mom cooking a large meal. Matthew and Susan join them, too.

Mark is a very welcoming host. He was a young widower when the Masters Clan first met him. He ran the Camp store at the Johnson Family Farm encampment that the family lived at during the picking of tomatoes, last year. When Anna did not show up at the diner that morning, Susan called Mark at the store and had him go to the Masters' Quonset hut to see if she was there. When everyone was alerted, he closed the store and they all started a search.

Mark, long had feelings for Melinda but did not have the nerve to approach her. During the tragedy, he was a rock for Melinda and Henry. During that year, apart, Henry spent all his days off roaming deserted territory, looking for her body. He would bring Matthew or Mark with him and they usually camped out and spent two days searching each time.

Matthew breaks out a deck of cards for a poker game. Judd, Frank, Mark and Henry all play while the ladies socialize. Matthew says, "Mark, are you ready to lose to me, this time?" He smiles as he said this. Mark was never a card player but Matthew has been playing with him since the long campout together and he has started to beat Matthew occasionally. "You have gotten pretty good. I must admit. You should sit down with us at the next big game."

Mark shakes his head. "Too high stake for me. I take no pleasure in the gamble. I just like take Melinda there, it feels like a date night."

Henry asks, "So Matthew, are you still going to the crap games, regularly?"

Matthew smiles, "How do you think I can afford my wife, my house and college? I do not make beans working as my father's right hand." He elbows his Pa.

"I can pay you in beans if you prefer." Judd threatens. "Grant is very generous in our salaries, I feel. You are just an ungrateful young' in."

"I miss your presence at the games, bro." Matthew says to Henry. "You taught me everything I know about craps and poker."

"Your skills have far exceeded the master, little bro." Henry and Matthew have been calling each other brother since the two families met up at the encampment two years ago.

Mark is the big winner of the night. Of course, no money exchanges hands, they're just playing for chips.

Anna feels very relaxed surrounded by her family. Mark's house was nice, but Melinda made it beautiful. She was never a homebody or liked housework or cooking. She was always looking for the next adventure. After her sister's disappearance, she discovered the quiet comforting love that Mark had to offer. She cannot believe that she would have disregarded Mark and anything that would tie her down before. She was even considering leaving the family and going off on her own to try new things and be on the wild side. Dealing with Anna's death changed her priorities. Nothing is more important than Love and Family. It was as if she was walking through her life with her eyes closed. When she opened them, there was her Mark.

Anna was looking at Susan. She was a blonde beauty. She comes from a well-to-do family and they gave a house to Susan and Matthew as a wedding present. Susan was instrumental in the capture of her cousin, John Walker. It was Susan that got him to confess, really. He wouldn't admit to anything until she baited him and kicked him in the broken nose. Anna says to Susan, "Have you seen John since he got out of prison?"

"No, he wouldn't dare come near me, or Matthew. He knows that he lost a cousin, the day he attacked you. I still cannot believe that he did it! I would have never thought it possible. I am very ashamed to be related to him." She looks down at her hands. "I am so glad that your brother and the family have never held me in contempt for being his kin. I love your family so much. I cannot imagine a day without Matthew in it.

He is everything to me."

"Welcome to true love!" Judy says. "It was those blue eyes that did it for me with Judd." Her husband has the clearest blue eyes. A trait that he passed to both Melinda and Matthew.

"It is like he is seeing me through my heart, mind and soul when he looks at me. That is what you said the first day, I met you." Susan says to Judy. "I feel that way, also."

"I do not think that has to do with the eye color as much as the connection of the heart. I feel the same feeling when Henry looks at me and he has grey eyes. His gaze warms my heart and makes it smile."

"We are all very lucky, I think. Good matches all around." Melinda says then changes the subject. "I hope that tomorrow goes well. What time do you need to be at the Courthouse?"

"The Trial begins at 10 a.m. but the District Attorney wants me in his office at 8 a.m. so we can go over the details before court." I hope I can sleep tonight, I am so nervous."

"Tell yourself that the baby needs you rested. Then count our blessings." Melinda says as she waves at the house full of their loving family.

TEN

Monday, October 4th, 1937
In EL Dorado, Kansas

The District Attorney wants to go over Anna's testimony. "I know it will be hard for you with all of us hearing the intimate details, but you did a great job testifying in front of the Grand Jury, two months ago. I do not see this being any harder, except for the fact John Walker will be there and that you will be cross-examined by the Defense Attorney. Remember, I can ask for breaks if it gets too much for you. As a matter of fact, the harder it is for you to get through it, the more the sympathy we will receive from the Jury."

Anna gives a half-hearted smile. "I think I can make it very sympathetic. He was brutal. Only a monster could do what he did to me."

He works with her for an hour and they still have time to kill, so Henry takes Anna to get coffee at Sally's Diner, where she worked for the week before she went missing. All the same waitresses were there and they hugged Henry and Anna and wished them well. They are at the Diner for about twenty minutes before they head back to the courthouse.

They have Anna and Henry wait outside the courtroom. Anna is shaking with nerves. Henry holds her hand. "You are going to do fine. Please just look at me as you tell what happened. You've done very well, so far. You did not falter with the district attorney; I am very proud of you." He leans in and kisses the side of her forehead.

The bailiff calls Anna to come in. Henry squeezes her hand for good luck and follows her into the courtroom.

Henry takes a seat on the side of the witness box so she can look at him directly. She looks very calm. Then he sees her gaze go to John at the Defendant's table. He sees her resolve dissolve and she looks beaten before the she utters a word.

She is sworn in and the Prosecuting Attorney ask her name, age and profession.

"My name is Anna Rose Masters Harrick. I am 21 years old and I am cook and a caretaker at the Legacy Plantation in Lawrence, Kansas."

"Mrs. Harrick, may I call you Anna?"

"Please do." She says with a small hint of a smile.

"Thank you, Anna. Let's get started. In 1935, you were abducted, assaulted and raped. Do you see the person who did this to you, in this Courtroom?"

She looks down at her hands, sighs deeply, and points to John Walker without looking at him.

"Who is it that you are pointing to, Anna?"

She still is pointing but she looks up at the Prosecutor. "John Walker kidnapped and raped me."

"In your own words, can you walk us through those events?"

"It was Saturday, the 28th of September in 1935. I was driving alone in my father's Ford truck, on my way to work at Sally's Diner. John Walker was pretending to have an overheated radiator. He was in the street waving me down. I was suspicious because I did not see any steam coming from his Model A. He asked if my sister, Melinda, was in the car. I told him no. He asked for water for his radiator but I did not have any. I told him that I was on my way to work, but that I would call someone for him when I got there.

"Suddenly, a large man was on my passenger side running board, then he opened the door and got in uninvited. He pulled me out of the driver's seat and opened the door for John to get in behind the wheel. He stayed only a second or two and he was out the door but he stayed on the running board for a few more moments. As soon as he left, John grabbed my hair styled in a bun for work, and slammed me into the dashboard. My forehead opened and blood streamed down my face. He wasn't satisfied, though, as I was pleading for help for the wound, he grabbed me a second time and pulled me back in such a way that as when he slammed me this time, my nose broke. I started to lose it from there, the pain was so blinding." Anna hesitated for a moment, trying to keep herself calm.

"He drove for quite a while. I remember seeing myself from above, in the cab of my father's truck bleeding and having a difficult time breathing. Occasionally, he would grab me again and my face would hit the dash again.

"When he got to the edge of the Lewis property, in Lawrence, he stopped driving and attempted to rape me in my father's truck. He ripped off my clothing and he wanted me to wipe up the blood streaming down my face and while trying to do so, I vomited onto the floor. He got so mad at me for that. He got out of the truck and pulled me out. He took my work pants from his side of the floor and told me to put them on my face so he couldn't see at me. He kept saying that he should have raped me when I was still beautiful. He held me down and did his business with no regard that I was a human being under him. He was belligerent and brutal. He kept telling me that he was going to kill me. He wanted to make Henry pay for an imagined offense, so he abducted me, mutilated me, raped me, and then ran me down with Pa's truck. I was so sure that I was going to die, and I hurt so bad that I wanted to. After the rape, he got in Pa's truck and drove off. I sat on the ground too weak to care if I lived or died. He was gone for a few minutes when I realized he was coming to run me down in my family's truck. I tried to run from the truck but I realized how foolish that was. There was nothing to hide behind. So, I faced him. I thought maybe he'd lose his nerve if he had to look me in the eye. The last thing I remember thinking was: I had a wonderful life and I thanked God for it."

She is barely holding back the tears now. She has not told Henry that last part. She was looking in his eyes for support but his eyes were misting over. Seeing Henry tearful, undid Anna. She looked over to John, "How could you have done this to me? I was always nice to you." She was on the brink of hysteria. Henry was on his feet. He wanted to go to her.

The Defense Attorney was on his feet, at the same time. "Your honor, please tell the witness not to address my client."

The Judge nods his head. "Mrs. Harrick, please do not address the Defendant.

Anna was not holding back. Tears were running down her cheeks. The Prosecutor looked at her with compassion. "Anna, I have no more questions for you but do you need a break before the Defense attorney starts his questioning?"

She nods. "Just a moment or two to collect myself, I think." She sobbed between words.

The Prosecutor looked to the Judge. "Your honor, can we have a fifteen-minute break?"

The Judge says, "There will be a fifteen-minute break. The witness will still be under oath and back in the witness chair when we reconvene." He pounds the gavel and Henry is on his feet again to go get Anna. The Prosecutor brings her to Henry. The Bailiff takes John out of the courtroom.

Henry walks her out to the hall. He hands her his handkerchief. "You did great, it is almost over. Do you need to use the restroom?" She blows her nose and instead of giving it back to him, she opens her purse and puts it inside.

"I think I will powder my nose, thank you, Henry." She kisses his cheek.

"For what?" He asks.

"You're here for me. You are my calm in the storm." He puts his arms around her.

"Hearing how close I came to losing you, makes me want to hold you and never let you go. John did the opposite of what he intended. I love you more now than ever, because you were taken from me, and -THANK YOU GOD - you came back to me." He kisses her on the forehead. "Now, go powder your nose." He pushes her toward the Ladies Room.

Once back on the stand, John's lawyer starts. "Anna, May I call you Anna?"

She shakes her head no. "I prefer you call me Mrs. Harrick. This way you remember that I am a married woman." She says with all seriousness.

The lawyer chuckles and says patronizingly. "Okay, MRS. Harrick. Can you tell me what happened on the Thursday and Friday before this alleged rape?"

Anna thought a moment. "I worked both of those days. And the rape was not alleged. It was real."

There was a snicker from John. Henry wanted to put his hands John's neck and strangle him.

"I was referring to the evening's events on those two

days, Mrs. Harrick." The lawyer continues, after he puts a hand on John's shoulder and squeezes a little to try and control him.

"What about them?" Anna asks, she was determined not to tell him anything unless he begs.

"Did you attend a floating crap game on Thursday night?"

"Yes"

"Did you see the merciless attack on my client at that game?"

"I did not. John was being very rude to everyone, and when I came back from the bathroom with my sister, John was on the floor. I did not see any of it."

"Didn't you let John buy you drinks, that night and the time before at the games?"

"John bought Henry and myself a drink at a previous night but on Thursday night when bought me a drink without asking, his cousin Susan took it from him. Henry was getting my drink, himself."

"I have another question for you, Mrs. Harrick. Is it true that you were not a virgin on the Saturday you went with Mr. Walker?"

"I did not 'go' with John. He kidnapped me. He did not give me a choice in the matter. Henry had proposed to me the night before and we got carried away. He was my intended. I was not a loose woman. I was in love." She says to the jury.

"Your honor, can you ask the witness to not address the jury and only answer just what I ask and not expand on it unless I ask her to?"

"You heard him, Mrs. Harrick. Please try to limit your answers to yes or no, unless asked for more."

"Yes sir, I will try." She looks down at her hands.

"Anna," the lawyer started to ask her another question.

Anna snaps to attention. "I prefer YOU call me Mrs. Harrick, please."

"Yes of course, sorry, MRS. Harrick. Isn't it true that your boyfriend, Henry, was seeing you and your sister romantically at the same time?"

"Not that I knew of." Anna didn't flinch, but her eyes went straight to her husband's, who looks away.

"Isn't it true that Henry and Melinda were meeting

nightly for romantic rendezvouses?"

"Not . . . that . . . I . . . knew . . . of!" She emphases each word and seems to be holding her breath.

"You did not know that Melinda was pretending to date my client to make Henry jealous, so he would pick her and not you?"

"No, I did not, and even if I did, what has that got to do with John raping me?" Her jaw was set as tight as could be, she was so upset.

"Your Honor, I have no further questions for this witness."

The Judge looks to the Prosecutor. "Mr. Pollack, do you want to redirect?"

"No, your honor. I have no other questions."

It was over. Anna was excused. She was trembling as she left the witness stand. Those things he was asking about Melinda and Henry, upset her. They should not have, because she remembers John telling her that Henry had the sisters 'dangling for a month', but Henry made his choice and has stuck to it through her 'dead' year and now a year of marriage. So why is she caught so off guard?

Henry met her in the aisle, and took her hand to walk her out of the courtroom. As soon as the doors closed behind them, Anna shook Henry's hand free from hers.

Henry knows that line of questioning reminded her of the lies that he and Melinda had told her. Anna hates lies and liars.

"I am sorry, Anna." Is all Henry can think to say. "I wish I could take back those weeks. I was very stupid. You are and have always been the only thing important to me." He tries to look in her warm brown eyes. "Anna, say something."

"I need to powder my nose, Henry. I will be right out." Without looking at him she walks away.

As she looks at herself in the mirror, her reflection looks tired and so different from the Anna before John Walker's attack. She had a heart shaped face and small nose. But now, her face is wider and her nose that had been fixed twice looks larger. She has a long scar on her forehead and a few smaller ones on her face. She knows that Henry truly loves her because he still thinks she is beautiful, even if John Walker did his best to erase everything beautiful about her. He is the real enemy, not Henry's momentary indecision.

She throws a little water on her face, dries it, straighten her shoulders in her convictions then goes out to her loving husband.

"Anna, the District Attorney said they might need you, again or me at some point but we do not need to wait around. This afternoon, they were going to hear from Dr. Mason, since he was the medical professional on the scene after the attack. We can go to Melinda's have lunch with Ma, Pa and Da and then head back to Lawrence, if you want. We will get called if something is needed or decided."

Henry takes her arm. She smiles up at him. "I would like that very much, Henry.

Henry, Anna and Frank drive back to Legacy Plantation early in the afternoon. They go straight to the Main house. Anna is worried about the Colonel. She knows that he can be a handful when she is not around to care for him.

Carolyn is in the kitchen. She has half of the contents out of the icebox and on the large marble island across from the stove. Anna and Henry enter from the back door and Anna looks around and exclaims, "What is going on here? Are you cleaning out the icebox or trying to make a meal?"

Carolyn is flummoxed. "Give me piece a of metal and welder, and I am in my element. Making meals for everyone is exhausting. How do you manage to make it so effortless?"

Anna looks around at the contents on the counter. "What was it you wanted to cook? You have several meats out." She walks to her frazzled adopted sister. "Why don't you just go make yourself useful somewhere else. I've got this." She puts her hands-on Carolyn's shoulders and turns her away from her.

"Wait, I want to hear about the trial. How did you do? Did you give that maniac a piece of your mind?" Carolyn spins back around. "Fill me in, on everything."

Henry speaks up. "She tried to yell at John but his lawyer stopped her. She did really well on the witness stand."

Anna cleans up the kitchen and begins the evening meal as she fills Carolyn on all the details of the day.

ELEVEN

October 4th, 1866. Thursday
An Excerpt from Elizabeth's Journal.

Last night, I woke up William as I restlessly tossed and turned in bed. I wanted to continue writing but I knew that I needed to get my rest. He asked if he could read what I wrote. I showed him what I had so far and he said he was very proud of me. He is such a sweetheart! I am very lucky to have someone who will support me.

Today, has been very busy. The Sunflower crop is in and we have day workers for the harvest. The fields should be cleared in just a few days, but it will be total chaos until then. Ian, Joseph and even little Willie help their father. Ian doesn't let one missing leg stop him from working just as hard as two-legged workers. I am very proud of my boy. Last year, we took Ian to the University of Kansas, Medical School and he was fitted for a wooden leg. It took him just a short time to get the hang of balancing on it, but he walks with a barely noticeable limp.

In my tale, I had just found out that William Quantrill was responsible for what was happening in the town. As I rode away from the business district, I tried to shield my daughter from seeing the dead bodies in doorways and on side streets. I could not understand what was going on.

I thought that I must go to the tent encampment where my boys slept, first. If I find them, I would not need confront Charlie. Devastation and torched houses were everywhere yet there were untouched houses in between. I hurried Nellie along Massachusetts Avenue as fast as I could make her go. There were lots of obstacles along the way. The bushwhackers were commandeering private buggies and buckboards to haul away all the items that they were stealing before they burned the owner's homes. We passed them, without being stopped or questioned, surprisingly.

When I turned east away from Mass Ave, I saw the encampment from afar. All the tents were in tatters and I could tell that many young bodies littered the ground.

I did not want to make Lizzie witness this disaster but we needed to continue to look for Ian and Joseph.

I did not know which end of the camp my boys stayed at. There were about twenty-two boys, all too young to be real soldiers, camped out here. It looked as if none survived the massacre. There were several parents here looking for their boys, also. Lizzie and I got down from the buckboard, (me with great difficulty) and started the horrible task of looking at all the dead faces, and talking to other parents. Some of the parents were calling names out loud hoping to find their loved one just injured and able to answer.

Lizzie stayed very close to me, throughout. She, suddenly, tugged my skirt and pointed to a Rebel who appeared to be standing guard over his work. He was allowing the parents to retrieve their sons, unmolested. Lizzie pointed and tugged again, then said in a whisper, "Isn't that Brownie, behind him?" It was my father's mare, she was right. I approached the bushwhacker and I was shaking when I asked if he knew where the rider of the mare was.

He just snickered, "Not able to ride her anymore." Then he pointed to the house behind me. On the porch, sat Father and young Willie. Father was shot in his right arm and holding Willie with his left.

When I saw Willie, I yelled to them. Willie left Father's side and ran to us. Apparently, Willie was not being held by Father but holding him up. My father slumped slightly to the left without the young one there to prop him up. I bent down and surveyed my boy, he had blood on him but none of it appeared to be his. "Are you hurt?" I asked him.

He shook his head no, then pointed to Father and said, "Papa's hurt, Mama." Before I could take a step forward, an evil laugh came from behind me. It was the Rebel.

"You don't need to get any closer, if you want the old man to live, Mrs."

I turned around instantly. "Please sir, my father isn't right in the head, he doesn't understand what is going on here. He couldn't hurt a fly, I promise."

Just then my father had a lucid moment and said with all clarity. "Beth, this is William Quantrill's army and they are going to kill all the men in the town. We knew him as Charlie Hart, remember?"

I was still facing the guerilla and he snickered, again. "He knows what is going on, perfectly. Doesn't he?"

"Well, even a broken clock is right twice a day!" I laughed, nervously. "He is unarmed and right handed. He has been shot in his shooting arm so he is no threat. Please let me take him. I was looking here for my two boys, before going to the Eldridge Hotel to speak with Colonel Quantrill. He is a friend of the family and wouldn't want us harmed."

"Is that so? Well, be assured that if your boys were in this camp, they are both dead. This was the first place we hit and no one survived. I cannot let you take the old man, especially if you are going to see the Colonel. What if he tried something?"

My heart was beating out of my chest. He said that my boys were dead! Tears welled up in my eyes. Lizzie started crying and then so did Willie. My father on the porch, struggled to get up and come to our aid.

"What did you say to my daughter, you ruffian? I will make you pay, for this!"

I could barely see, through my tears, but the Rebel raised his rifle and before I could say anything, he pointed it at us. "Don't move an inch closer, old man. I do not want to kill them if you _are_ a friend of the Colonel, but I cannot have you threatening me!"

Without turning to him, I said, "Father, please." I put my hand out as a signal to stop. "We are safe, we are friends with Charlie, remember? He used to hold Willie and take tea with Lizzie?"

The bushwhacker started to laugh. Then he laughed harder. "Took tea with Lizzie? The Colonel? Now I know you are lying! The Colonel hates tea!" He raised the rifle higher and pointed it at Father, now.

Father must have moved, I think. He started to say, "My daughter is no liar. Charlie . . ." but he did not finish his sentence. The rifle went off and Father was shot in the chest. I turned in time to see him stumble backwards a few steps, back to the porch and fall on it.

I ran to him. "Father, no!!" I tried to hold him up. "Please Father don't die. I couldn't handle it if you died as well as my boys!" I wailed. My father moved his left hand and I saw the handgun in it. Did the Rebel know he was armed? I reached for the gun and struggled with it. It was too big to be hidden. I put it in my skirt waist, then pulled my shawl tight to hide it. Father whispered something. I bent down to hear it.

"Kill the Son of a Bitch, Beth. Do it now, he isn't expecting it." I rose from his side. Father coughed a few times from the effort of talking. His body went slack and I knew that he was breathing his last. I angrily wiped my tears so that I could see my target and I turned to face the man that just killed my Father.

He was holding both Willie and Lizzie, by the collars of their clothing. Both were struggling to get away. Since both his hands were occupied, I knew this was the time to shoot. Almost without thinking, I pulled the gun from my skirt waist, aimed at his head and fired. The impact of the bullet pushed him backwards and he fell, dead but still holding my little ones. They fell with him then both screamed because he had only half a face. They ran to me and held me tight.

The townspeople who were looking for their son's bodies came up to me to thank me for killing one of the men who shot their boys. I asked if they would help me put my father in the buckboard. We continued the search of the dead and no one could find my boys, so once again, I climbed up into the buckboard with Lizzie and Willie. I needed to talk with Charlie. My father-in-law Clyde and my Uncle Daniel, as well as the boys were still missing. He must help us.

TWELVE

Tuesday, October 5[th,] 1937
In Lawrence, Kansas

Anna wakes up before the first light. She is in Henry's arm. She sighs. This is her happy spot. She knows that yesterday, she had felt unsure of herself and Henry. He has more than made up for that brief time he dated both her and Melinda in secret. He had explained that he had asked Melinda out before their fathers had the talk that arranged their marriage. Henry said that he was just trying to push the limits of independence. He was against anything his father wanted. And Da wanted him to marry Anna. He shortly realized that his father was right.

Anna, Henry and Frank go to the Main house to begin the day's work. It felt great to get back to normal. She wanted to put John Walker and the trial as far behind her as is possible. Henry had insisted that since her pregnancy and the trial were going to happen at the same time, she was not to be at it, unless testifying. She would have argued the matter but she didn't want to see John Walker ever again.

Breakfast and lunch both come and go without incident. After lunch, Carolyn mentions Elizabeth's Journals. "The Colonel said that he remembered his mom shooting that Rebel. Can you believe that? I would like to get these published at some point. We should have a family get-together and I can present them to my great-aunts and great-uncles. I think I'll start calling the relatives and see if come for the Colonel's birthday party."

The Colonel has been asking for Henry's father, yesterday and today. He said that Julia has come up with the idea that Da could help him up and down, so Anna would not have to in her condition.

Da loves the idea. "The Colonel is a very sweet soul. I love feeling useful."

Henry is about to go back out to the sunflower fields. The heads should be ready tomorrow, according to Joshua. The spraying that they did a few days ago controlled the bug infestation. There will be dozens of pickers working and they should have the four acres picked in no time.

Just then the phone rings and all them make a move to answer it. Carolyn laughs, "I got it." She goes into the dining room where the first-floor phone is located. "Lewis Residents, Carolyn speaking. Yes, Henry is right here, hang on." She goes back into the kitchen. "Henry, it's for you, and it isn't Matthew"

The only one who calls Henry is Anna's brother, so Henry is very curious as to who it can be. He goes into the dining room to the side board where the phone is kept. He does not know it, but Anna is following close behind him. "This is Henry, how can I help you? . . . Yes, Mr. Pollack, I can . . . of course, we can . . . okay, see you then. Have a good night. Sir."

Henry places the receiver on the cradle, and when he turns he is surprised to see Anna. "They want me to testify on Thursday. Doesn't that beat all! They told me that they didn't want the story of my punch to be introduced. They did not want to give him justification for his actions."

"I was careful not to mention it in my testimony. But then the Defense Attorney asked me about . . . how did he put it, 'the merciless attack'? I bet they are basing their defense on that punch."

"I think they should call Susan to the stand. She can testify to how horrible he was at the Crap game and how I wanted her to tell her cousin that I was sorry for my actions. Let me call Mr. Pollack, back and suggest that." He turns back to the phone.

Anna goes back to the kitchen, worried again about the trial. Now they must go back to EL Dorado. Joshua was counting on Henry to help organize the sunflower workers, and control the chaos. "Oh, when will life just run smoothly?" She asks her little one in her belly.

Henry comes back in, "Don't upset the babe, Anna. There is nothing to worry about. I will go in on Wednesday night, stay with Matthew, testify in the morn and be back by sunset on Thursday night. You know, I don't want to miss a night of Beth's story!"

THIRTEEN

October 5ᵗʰ, 1866. Friday
An Excerpt from Elizabeth Lewis's Journal

When I got to the Hotel, there were three bushwhackers standing guard outside of the building. My Lizzie climbed down and was trying to help me down. The youngest looking rebel left his post and came to assist me down. After both my feet were on stable ground, I straightened my shoulders and asked if Colonel Quantrill was on the premises. The two guards at the door just laughed at me.

The young one said, "Ma-am, he is inside but is holding court, as it were. I do not think he wants to entertain visitors."

"But I must speak to him, he knows me from when he was here three years ago. He knows my boys and would not want to see them hurt. It's imperative that I speak with him. Tell him Mrs. Elizabeth Lewis, from the Laundry is here, please. Tell him that I have little Lizzie and young Willie with me to see him, too. He will want to see us, I promise." I was on the verge of tears, again.

The boy smiled (he looked around Ian's size and age) and turned to enter the Hotel. The two at the doorway tried to block his way. "Come on, Guys, Colonel will be mad if he knew a friend of his was denied entrance. Do you want to make him mad?"

They stood aside and I and the little ones waited, while he went in to plead our case. We could still hear random shots, shouts and screams all about the town, and I am sure that new fires were being started, too. I tried to remain calm. My heart was racing. The men in my life were in peril. William was in the War. Ian, Joseph, my Father-in-law, and Uncle were all out here in harm's way. I need to talk sense to Charlie. I mean the Colonel. As I stood there, suddenly the baby moved, then moved again. It was very uncomfortable. I started feeling pressure in my womb. The babe cannot think of coming right now! This is the worst time! I shifted my weight and hugged my belly with one hand and tried to squeeze Lizzie's hand with the other to reassure her. I then held my breath, then panted as quietly as I could. But, Lizzie knew something was happening.

"Mama, is it the baby? Are you in pain? It's too early to be your time, isn't it?" Her voice sounded small and scared.

A deep voice spoke from the staircase. "Mrs. Lewis, are you unwell? Let's get you inside. Shall we? Would a cup of tea and a comfortable chair help?" William Quantrill aka Charlie Hart stood in front of me, looking concerned. "Please Mrs. Lewis, let me help you." He bends slightly to my daughter. "Miss Lizzie, is it you, young lady? You've grown so big! Do you remember me? It's Charlie!" He did not wait for a reply but stood back up and took my hand, put it on his arm and led me into the Hotel. The young Rebel accompanied us, looking very worried, too.

Charlie has aged quite a bit in the three short years since I saw him last. He was barely twenty-six years old but looked closer to forty. He was freshly bathed, shaven and had waxed his mustache. He even had a manicure! He was doing the best he could, to show everyone that he was no longer a border ruffian and two-bit thief. He walked us past the front parlor and took us to a private small conference room. He motioned to a kitchen servant and ordered tea and sweet cakes to be sent to the room.

He settled us in then asked, "Mrs. Lewis, is this my young Willie?" He ruffed up Willie's hair. Willie swatted at him, and clung to Lizzie. "He must be a little terror! My best memories of this town were of holding him as a babe and playing Tea with Miss Lizzie, here." He smiles at her and she returns it.

"I remember having tea with you. Then you just left. I was very sad when you did that." She blushes and lowers her gaze in embarrassment.

The smile he had for her left his face, as he turned to me and said, "How may I be of service, Mrs. Lewis?"

"Charlie, I mean Colonel Quantrill, it's about my boys. Ian and Joseph are in danger out there. Your men do not know them. I do not know where they are and I am so worried." I rushed out my words. My pains had started and I needed to get my sentence out before I had the next contraction.

"Why weren't they home on the farm, safe and sound with you and your husband?" He asks genuinely concerned.

"My William is . . . um is away in the Cavalry and Ian and Joseph were in the Kansas Regiment for young soldiers. My Father got away from me and took young Willie to look for them, first. You remember how my Father was sick, don't you? He was already showing signs of confusion years ago, remember?" I started to cry. "He and Willie snuck out to the encampment to look around and my father was killed by one of your men. His dead body is in my buckboard. I searched the whole encampment for Ian and Joseph. Can you help me find my boys?" I knew that confessing that we were Union supporters, with opposite beliefs of his was dangerous, but if I remembered one thing about Charlie it was that, he hated liars! This was a huge gamble but as I sat there knowing the time for my confinement at hand, I had to cut corners. Before Charlie could answer in any way, my water broke and I felt myself blush then panic.

Charlie noticed. He calmly got up and went to the door to call the servant woman. Then he and the Rebel boy exchanged a few sentences.

The boy looked to me and smiled. "At your service, ma-am! My name is Jesse James and I will go find your boys. Ian and Joseph, are they? I will find them, promise. Don't you worry, none." He gave a little bow to me and left.

"Mrs. Lewis, I think we need to get you to a room with a bed. Do you think you can go up the stairs?" Charlie came to me and allowed me to lean on him to rise. I know that I keep calling William Quantrill - Charlie but he will always be that to me. I did feel very faint upon standing. As I started to swoon, I felt Charlie gently sweep me off my feet and carry me up the stairs.

Lizzie was very calm, for a ten-year-old. "Mr. Charlie, Mama is gonna need a mid-wife or doctor. I know that Nathan Stone's brother Dr. Leonard is staying at the City Hotel. Can you get him here, or let me go get him?" She blushed again and looked down.

"You stay with your Mama and Willie. I will see what I can do, Miss Lizzie. Don't you worry. Did I ever tell you that you remind me of my little sister Mary? She is still in Ohio."

"Yes sir, I remember you said that she was a seamstress."

"That's right, Miss Lizzie, you have a good memory, don't you?" Charlie said as he carried me effortlessly to an upstairs bedroom and put me on the bed. I was still light-headed but very warm at the same time. I know that I had beads of perspiration on my brow. Charlie walked over to the water pitcher and wet a towel and gave it to Lizzie and told her to put that on my forehead. Then he excused himself and left. I did not know if I was going to have the baby alone in this hotel room or if he was indeed going to help me.

That young Jesse looked earnest when he said that he would find my boys. I did not know at that time what a desperado he would turn out to be, after the war!

I started removing some of my outer garments. This being my fifth child, I knew what was ahead of me. Lizzie helped me maneuver. Forty minutes or so passed. Finally, there was a small knock on the door and two older women came in, laden with linens and cloths. They were patrons of the Hotel and though the Raiders had made the guests evacuate to the City Hotel, they were brought back because they were each a mid-wife in their day. What a relief, I thought for a while that my ten-year-old daughter would have to deliver my baby.

FOURTEEN

Thursday, October 7th, 1937
In EL Dorado, Kansas

Henry is at the District Attorney's office at 8 am to discuss his testimony. He stayed at Matthew's last night and brought Susan with him, today. She will also be testifying. Anna didn't want him to go to EL Dorado without her but EVERYONE at the Lewis house and ALL her relatives in EL Dorado insisted that she not subject herself to the possibility of seeing her attacker again.

The D.A. in charge, Mr. Pollack, wants Henry to explain how sorry he was about punching John that Thursday night at the Crap Game. Henry says, "I am sorry about that punch, then and now. I should have killed him instead. I should testify to that."

Mr. Pollack laughs, "Let's leave the talk of murder out of the courtroom today if you can, Mr. Harrick. I do not think it will help our case."

They were in the hallway outside of the courtroom when Susan offers, "I tried to call John on Friday to pass along Henry's apology but . . ." She stopped walking and talking. The Defense Attorney is leading John into the courtroom.

"Well, isn't this cozy. Henry and my former cousin Susan. Come to testify against me, Susan? I do not know how they have brainwashed you, so completely. Blood is thicker than water!" He shouts that last part because he is being pulled into the courtroom.

"Nothing like a family reunion to brighten the morning!" Susan says in a lilting tone.

Henry smiles at her and puts a protective arm around her shoulders. "The crazy part is he thinks we are the ones in the wrong here."

Once again, Henry is sitting on the bench outside of the courtroom waiting for the bailiff to come out. He and Susan are holding hands. She is shaking.

The bailiff calls Henry into the courtroom, he is sworn in and he sits down in the witness seat.

"Please state your name, age and profession, sir." The Prosecuting Attorney begins.

"Henry Harrick, sir, twenty-two years of age and I am an Assistant Farm Manager at The Legacy Plantation, where John Walker attempted to kill my Anna."

"Objection, your Honor, the defendant is not on trial on those charges."

"He should be!" Henry manages to get in.

The Judge's gavel strikes, "That's enough, Mr. Harrick, please keep your answers to the questions asked and make them as concise as you can."

"Yes, sir, I will try."

"May I call you Henry?" Asks the D.A.

"By all means."

"Henry can you tell me the events on the Thursday before your wife was attacked?"

"I went to a floating Crap game with Anna. Her siblings were there, already. John was supposed to be Melinda Masters' date but he did not show up to bring her, himself, so her brother Matthew drove her. Once we got there, John tried to buy Anna a drink, again, but refused to buy one for his 'date', until his cousin Susan chided him.

"He was being very belligerent to all the Masters and me. He was being a bully. He was trying to get me in trouble with Anna by hinting that I was seeing her sister Melinda. The truth is that I did see them both for a few weeks before I realized my total devotion to Anna."

"What exact thing did he say that led to your right hook?"

"He asked what did Anna have that Melinda didn't? I answered that Anna has my heart and that Melinda and I are friends. Then he said something like 'Ain't that cute, Anna has your heart. So, what did Melinda have, your COCK?' What would you do if someone said that to you, I ask?"

"I think I would have reacted in a similar way. Please go on, tell the jury exactly how you reacted."

"Without thinking, I took a swing at him and I must have connected just right, he went down like a rock. The bouncers came running, they thought he was a drunk, passed out. The two of them each grabbed an arm to remove him from the premises. He woke up while they were dragging him out and started cursing me out and threatening me. 'I'll make you pay, Henry, I'll make you pay!' were his exact words.

"Thank you, Mr. Harrick, I have no more questions, at this time."

The Defense Attorney rises and walks to Henry. "Henry, I have a few questions for you. If you don't mind."

"Please call me, Mr. Harrick." Henry smiles. Anna did the same thing and he thought it was just the perfect thing to do.

"Okay, Mr. Harrick, is it true that you were dating both sisters at the same time?"

"I've already admitted to that."

"Isn't it true that Melinda was dating you and John Walker at the same time?"

"You need to ask Melinda about that."

"Isn't it true that you threatened my client on more than on occasion before the Crap Game punch?"

"Not that I can recall."

"When your brother-in-law was going to work with John, did you or did you not, threaten him to keep Matthew safe?

"A threat is only a threat if one takes it as such. John said that I did not scare him. I believed him. I did not want his influence getting Matthew into deeper trouble."

"Isn't it true, Mr. Harrick, that you were sleeping with both sisters and keeping their affection for yourself and talking against my client?"

"Melinda and I were over before I had relations with my wife Anna."

"And what about giving John a bad name to the sisters and his cousin Susan?"

"He did that all by himself. You might say he was proficient at it so he needed no help from me."

"I'd like to ask you about the events on the day of your Fiancée's disappearance. Did you or did you not force yourself into my client's home?"

"We knew his vehicle was seen on the road where Anna went missing so we went to question him."

"I asked if you forced your way in? You did not have permission to enter, did you?"

"His cousin Susan had permission and we

accompanied her. He was manhandling Susan so we intervened. It wasn't necessary, though, we found out Susan can take care of herself." Henry smiled at the memory.

"Isn't it true that your two brothers-in-law held my client down on the floor and tied him up, before you beat him and stabbed him?"

"All this took place after he attacked Anna. We were trying to find out where he took her. I would have done anything to him to get Anna back."

"Your Honor, please tell the witness to answer the questions asked." The Defense Attorney said.

"Mr. Harrick, you must cooperate, when asked a question, please answer it. I will not tell you, again." The Judge warns.

"Yes, your Honor, I will try."

"I believe my question was: "Isn't it true that your two brothers-in-law held my client down on the floor and tied him up, before you beat him and stabbed him?"

"I never beat him, but I did try to cut his throat after he said, 'Thanks to me, she will never look the same. Your beautiful Anna is dead and gone!' When he said that, I wanted to gut him like a fish, but Melinda held me back. She pleaded with him to tell us where her body was."

"Objection, your Honor. A forced confession of Anna's murder should not be allowed. My client is not on trial for murder, and Anna is not now, nor has she ever been dead!"

"Over-ruled. You asked a question as to Mr. Harrick's feelings and actions. So, asked and answered. Move on, Mr. Delaney."

"No more questions for this witness, your honor." Mr. Delaney says.

"Mr. Pollack, do need to redirect?"

"Yes, I would, your Honor. Mr. Harrick, let me ask you this. Do I have these events correct? 1.) Mr. Walker was dating Melinda. 2.) He coerced Matthew (a minor at the time) to be the driver of a robbery. 3.) He tried to buy Anna drinks on more than one occasion, while she was your date. 4.) Mr. Walker's vehicle was seen at the site where Anna was abducted. 5.) Mr. Walker said to you and other witnesses that he stopped her in the street that morning. 6.) Mr. Walker admitted to you and other witnesses that 'thanks to him, Anna will never look the same.' Are all those events true and in the order in which I stated them?"

"You got it right, a hundred percent."

"Thank you, Mr. Harrick, I am finished with you, you may be excused. Your Honor, due to the lateness of the morning, may we break for lunch before I call my next witness?"

"Good idea, Mr. Pollack. This court is recessed for one and a half hours for lunch. I want all parties back here at 1 pm ready to start."

Henry leaves the witness stand and the courtroom. Susan is still on the bench where he left her. "We are on break, we have time to go to the Diner, if you like, my treat."

"I do not know if I can eat anything. Between morning sickness and nerves, I am lucky that I have not given back my breakfast!" They start walking toward the exit, when she stops, suddenly. "In fact, I am not feeling well, at all." She runs to the Ladies Room.

Henry is standing waiting for her, when the D.A. comes out of the courtroom. Henry stops him. "You might not have a witness available this afternoon. The little missus, is with child and the babe is making her very ill. Is there anyone else, you can call? Melinda, maybe or how about the accessory. John's friend, Pete, was the one who helped John abduct Anna. He is serving time for the Paymaster Heist, right now.

District Attorney Pollack thinks on this for a moment. "We have offered him immunity from being the accomplice for his testimony. Good thinking, Henry. Why don't you take Susan home? I will arrange for Pete's testimony. If I cannot get him down for this afternoon, I can just ask the Judge for a continuance."

When Susan came out of the Ladies Room, Henry explained the new strategy. Susan said, "What a relief! I will still testify at some point, I imagine. Hopefully, it will be a day that Matthew can miss class. Thank you, Henry, you've been great."

Henry asks, "Are you well enough for the Diner, now? My offer still stands, my treat. You do look much better since you've come out of the Ladies room."

"Only because I gave back my breakfast! Now I am starving. Let's hit Sally's, then you can just drop me off and head back to Lawrence. I know you do not want to be away from Anna, another night."

FIFTEEN

October 7th, 1866. Sunday
An Excerpt from Elizabeth Lewis's Journal
In Lawrence, Kansas

Several days have passed since I last wrote. Too much work and not enough hands to do it. The Sunflowers are near all picked and for most of them, we are taking the seeds out of the heads for salting and slow roasting. This is very arduous work but the Sweet Shop pays us handsomely for the gems once cooked, cooled and in small barrels. Sunflower seeds are a small salty delicacy that Lawrence is becoming known for and the only place to get them is the Sweet Shop. It will take about a week to get them all processed and delivered.

My laundry lady employees help me with this endeavor. None of them were physically harmed in the Massacre, but two of them lost their husbands and all their employment. They help me here whenever I need them.

This town has more than survived the Massacre, it has flourished because of it. Most of the business district has been rebuilt. Wagon loads of people, produce, and lumber came into town immediately after the word spread about the Massacre. The first problem was to bury all the dead (and dying). We did not have enough caskets. At a town meeting, it was decided not have a mass grave site but each and every person would be buried with honor and dignity, when possible. The call for caskets and the lumber went out and was answered swiftly. Even though Missouri was our enemy and harbored Quantrill's men for years before the Massacre, they supplied half of the lumber needed to bury our dead. But this was before the Ewing General Order No. 11 which evacuated and burned all the Missouri homes in a fifteen-mile swath along the Kansas border. Thousands of people lost their homes during this forced evacuation.

It pains me to talk of the burying the dead. We had three to bury. I thank God my boys were alive but I still mourn and grieve for my baby girl, my father and my

Uncle and I am still racked with guilt. If I did not go to town that day, of all days, my baby and Father might both be alive.

Back in that little room in the Eldridge Hotel, I was enduring the worst pain of my life. I had been through the birthing process four times before, but this one was, by far, the hardest. I was very mad at the little one for picking the worst time to make its entrance. I needed to find my boys! Why was this happening now? Mrs. Caldwell and Miss Petrie were very calm and understanding. I was crying out loud at the helplessness of my situation. Mrs. Caldwell tried to tell me that I was upsetting the babe in the womb with my anxiousness thus causing more pain to myself. But the pain was causing my anxiousness! After two hours of labor, I was no farther along the delivery than the hour before. I knew that the longer the babe stayed in the dry womb the worst the chances of it being stillborn or a 'slow' baby. My cousin Sara, took five hours from the water breaking to the birth and her son's brain was damaged.

Suddenly, I had another pain from the child. "Ooohh! Why here, why now? I am not due for weeks!" Miss Petrie put a fresh cloth on my forehead, while I ranted and raved, beside myself with worry and grief.

A short time later, a knock came and Charlie asked to come in. The two women told him no, but he insisted. I was barely aware of his presence.

"Mrs. Lewis, I gave Ms. Petrie a little laudanum to help ease your pain. I have had multiple people looking for your two boys with no luck at all. I am so sorry. I do think that it is a _good_ sign that their bodies have not been found. Mrs. Lewis, I wish there was more that I could do for you. My time is done here, and my men and I will be leaving. My dear Mrs. Lewis, you and your little family and Nathan Stone's family were the only people in this horrible town that meant anything to me. I should have come to you first to make sure that you were safe through this. I sincerely regret that my inaction put you and your family in harm's way. I wish you all the best, Mrs. Lewis, with all my heart." With that he excused himself and retreated out of the room before I had a chance to give him a piece of my mind.

As the door closed, the most I could managed to say

was "good riddance!" before my agony resumed. Mrs. Caldwell put a few drops of laudanum in an ounce of water and made me drink it. I was only awake for a few minutes after that.

SIXTEEN

Friday, October 8th 1937
In EL Dorado, Kansas

The District Attorney had already made a deal with inmate Pete Sullivan. He had told him that he could face new charges of Abduction, Assault and Accessory to Rape. He convinced him that good testimony against John Walker could undo all that. Pete harbored no loyalty to Walker and he was able to get him transferred to the court so he testified on Thursday afternoon in the place of Susan.

Susan and Matthew are at the District Attorney's office at 8 a.m. Matthew knows most of the lawyers in the office from his time testifying against Harry, and Pete for the Paymaster Robbery. His familiarity, makes Susan more at ease.

"Mr. Pollack, it is nice to see you again. How are the proceedings looking so far? Anna and Henry told us about their testimony. Sounds like they did well."

"I am very hopeful about this case. We have Pete's testimony, Dr. Mason's, the retired sheriff Lark Bailey, and you, Susan and Melinda have yet to testify. I do not know what kind of defense they will have. It cannot be much of one."

"I still cannot believe that John is out free during the trial. He did such a heinous thing to my sister. I have never met a more unstable person." Matthew admits.

"You are very young, Matthew, there is still time for you to meet other evil people in the world, but I hope that you will not. Susan, how are you feeling, today? You are glowing, my dear. Ready to testify?

"Yes sir. I think I will be fine, today. I am usually ill around lunch-time for some reason. I do not know why they call it morning sickness."

"I do not know either. But as long, as we can get you in before the sickness sets in. It will not help or hinder our case if you get sick on the stand. I just don't think that will be pleasant for any of us."

"I wouldn't mind if she does it as she passes John

and projects it to him." Matthew quips.

"Oh, Matthew. What a thing to say. I can almost picture it. Of course, anything is possible." She says with a smile. "Can Matthew be in the courtroom during my testimony?" Susan asks shyly.

"Well, I think not. We will be calling him right after you. We want his testimony fresh and unbiased by what you say on the stand."

"Oh, I thought since Anna had Henry in the courtroom, I could also."

"Henry and Anna gave testimony on different areas of the case. And we could tell Anna, could not have gotten through the intimate details without her husband's support. Your testimony is much more general than that. We are going to ask you about John's mother's death and how he handled being fired from the oil company for taking care of her before she died. We are also going to ask you about his attitude after the Paymaster robbery but before the Punch. Also, we will ask you about his interrogation at his house. I understand that you were instrumental in his confession."

Matthew interrupts, "I knew I loved her the moment she kicked John in his broken nose. She was adamant that he knew something. We had very little to go on, but she knew him better than us and insisted that his answers were not the whole truth. We couldn't have done it without Susan."

"That's when you knew you loved me? While I was part of the John Walker interrogation team? Not when I batted my eyes for you at the poker game? I do not know how I feel about that." She laughs. "I fell in love with you the first time you asked me to blow on your dice, at that Thursday night Crap Game. I even told your mother that the first time I met her."

"Isn't it enough that I AM in love with you?" Matthew kisses his bride on the forehead, then changes the subject. "What will I be testifying about?"

"John's attitude against Henry from the beginning. How John got you in as the get-a-way driver for the Paymaster robbery and the interrogation and the wild goose chase that he put everyone on to find Anna's body. How he led you nowhere near where he last saw her, on what we now know, was the Lewis property in Lawrence."

They head to the courtroom and as they get nearer Susan begins to shake again. Then the bailiff comes out of the courtroom and calls her name. "Oh Matthew, I am very nervous. I do not know how you did this, three different times. I am all raw nerves."

"Susan, if Anna could do it with what her testimony revealed, and looking at the man who mutilated and raped her, you can also. You have known John your whole life. Just answer the questions calmly and try to remember to breathe before you answer. I forgot a few times on the stand and nearly died from it." He is making fun of her now and she knows it.

"Such a goofy kid, you are, my husband." Matthew bends down and gives her a kiss on the cheek.

"A kiss for luck, my dear. Now go get him."

Susan is on the stand and sworn in. She gives her name age and profession. "My name is Susan Walker Masters; I am nineteen-years-old and I am a part-time librarian at the EL Dorado Public Library."

"Mrs. Masters, are you related to the defendant?" The Prosecuting Attorney starts.

"Unfortunately, I am John's first cousin and the thought of it sickens me."

"Good one Susan, it sickens me also!" John blurts out.

"Objection, your honor."

"Mrs. Masters, please leave your opinions to yourself unless asked for them." The Judge says then turns to Mr. Delaney and warns, "Keep your client in control, Counselor, or I will have him removed from the courtroom."

"I will try, your honor." Mr. Delaney says while Susan answers, "Yes, sir." She says this barely above a whisper.

"Mrs. Masters, you've known Mr. Walker, your whole life. Can you talk about his mother's death?"

"My Aunt Molly got very sick from the dust storm that everyone calls Black Sunday in April of 1935. My Aunt was diagnosed with dust influenza. She slowly choked to death from the dust in her lungs. It was not a peaceful death. John was devoted to her care. When she became, bed ridden, John left his job at the oil refinery to take care of her. He was home less than a week but the oil refinery would not take him back. He told everyone that he will make them pay. He went off the deep end. Mumbling, tearing things apart in his mother's home, where he lived. We thought it was simple grief at first but it seemed to be more. He said that he blamed the oil company for her death, because he wanted to stay home with her sooner, if he had she might be alive. Nothing could be further from the truth but John has his always had his own way of thinking."

"You know he was involved in the Paymaster robbery at the Johnson Farm. What was his demeanor and attitude afterward?"

"He didn't show up for work on the fields. And he was spending money like it was dry dirt, saying that he got lucky at poker or something. I was at most the games that he was at and he did not play poker at any of them. He would brag and lie about the most ridiculous things. He had it bad for Melinda, well for a week or two. Then Henry brought Anna to the games. He was in awe of her. He told me once that she was pure perfection and too good for Henry." She looks at her cousin. "How could you mutilate something you thought was perfect? How could your hate twist you like that?" Susan got very red in the face.

"Your Honor!" Mr. Delaney calls out. "She is talking to my client. Why does everyone want to talk to my client?"

"Mrs. Masters, please limit your comments. Answer the questions only. Do NOT address the defendant." The Judge barks.

Mr. Pollack continues. "Mrs. Masters, could you take us through the events that led to the questioning of John Walker?"

"I was supposed to make a few calls for Anna, for her quick wedding to Henry. She was working six days a week so she needed to buy a dress and get her hair cut and I had recommendations for both, but I did not know if they would be open on Sunday, which was her only day off. Well, I went to Sally's Diner at 2 p.m. to tell her about my phone calls. She was supposed to be working from nine to six but she did not show up for work. I knew that she was expecting me and that she loved her job. Anna would never just <u>not</u> show up. Well, I called Mark Collins who works at the encampment where she lived, to find out if she was home. Her family was shocked but sprang into action. Melinda got Henry's dad to go get Henry and Matthew from the tomato field. I drove to the encampment to see if she had a breakdown with her father's Ford truck. We tried to call John from the Camp Store but John did not answer.

Mark closed the store and we split up to look for Anna and file a missing person report. I let Matthew take my car with his Pa and they did that while I sat with his Ma, Judy. She was in an awful way. She had a premonition that she would not see Anna ever again. Well, Mark and Melinda kept going over the route that Anna took and they asked people that they saw if they saw anyone on the road from 7:30 a.m. They found a witness that they saw a Model A with a tall man, who was Pete, and a short stocky man, which would have been John. That was enough for Matthew and Henry, they knew the Model A was the car that was used in the Paymaster job, and it was John's secret car. They decided that it was time to go confront John.

I went up onto the front porch, and knocked a few times. He finally answered the door but he was drunk and grabbed me by my hair and dragged me into his house. Just as I went to fight back, Matthew had gotten in from the back door and he tackled him to the floor. We tied him up and we kept asking him about Anna. He was saying that he wouldn't tell us anything. I knew that meant that he had something to tell. I got so mad that I gave him a swift kick and I guess, I got his broken nose again. Mark to took me to cool off into the kitchen and to call the Sheriff.

When the sirens got closer to the house, I went to the front door and I heard John admit to mutilating and killing Anna. He left her for dead and it was nothing short of a miracle that she did not die. After the sheriffs came and put John into the ambulance, we were questioned then they told us all to go home. Melinda thought about the missing Ford Truck and I said to look in John's garage, and there it was. Pa's truck with the broken headlamp with Anna's hair and blood still attached. There was blood and Anna's clothing and vomit inside the truck. John did not try to clean anything or hide anything. He . . . He . . . He . . ." Susan suddenly looks green. "I need to . . . oh, why did I mention Anna's vomit?"

The D.A. brought a garbage can with him to assist Susan off the stand. She waved it away and just ran out of the courtroom. Just outside the door was Matthew and he jumped up and ran with her into the Ladies Room.

The D.A. looked up at the Judge. "Sorry, your honor, Mrs. Masters is newly with child and she suffers from . . . it. May we take a little break?"

"Apparently, we already are taking a break. We will adjourn for fifteen minutes. I hope your witness will be composed enough to continue. We must give the Defense a chance to question her." He bangs his gavel.

Fifteen minutes later, Susan was back in the stand looking just slightly less green. Matthew had argued that she should not continue but Susan said that she needs to finish this. The bailiff called the court to order and the Judge came back to his seat.

"Mrs. Masters are you better? Can you continue?" The Judge asks her.

"I am a little better, your Honor, thank you for asking. I will try to finish without another interruption." Susan says as she blushes red over her green.

"We do understand that you are in a delicate condition. Congratulations." The Judge smiles at her.

"Now I am going to be sick!!" John blurts again. The Judge whips his attention around and glares at John.

"This is your last outburst, Mr. Walker. You will be removed from these proceedings the next time you open your mouth without being sworn in and on the witness-stand, yourself. Do you understand the gravity of my words? You will not be able to participate in your defense if you are not in the room. So be fair warned." He turns to the Prosecuting Attorney. "Mr. Pollack, please continue."

"Mrs. Masters, is there any doubt in your mind as to whether your cousin could and did these things he is accused of?"

"Without a shadow of a doubt, John Walker abducted her, assaulted her, raped her and left poor Anna Masters for dead. In my opinion and in my gut, I know these things to be true." She was near tears and looks down at her hands as she gains control of her emotions.

"I have no further questions for this witness, your honor. You did well, Susan." Mr. Pollack turns to sit down at his table.

"Mr. Delaney, you may cross-examine the witness." Says the Judge.

"Mrs. Masters, I will try to be brief, so as not to tax you in your delicate condition. You accompanied John to these floating crap games several times before meeting the Master family and Henry Harrick. Did you or did you not?"

"I did, we were doing that for a year or so."

"So you were using John before you found a new patsy to take you?"

"We used each other. John liked having me on his arm when we walked in to these places."

"You testified to John caring for his mother. How long did he do that?"

"His whole life. Aunt Molly was a sickly woman. Black Sunday was on April 14th 1935. She got very sick right away after that. John took care of everything for his mother. She passed away in June, so for three months she was really bad."

"Did anyone else take care of her?"

"My mother as a nurse, would check in on her four days a week. But I do not think John had anyone else come into the house."

"So in your estimation, John was caring, patient and loving."

"At that time, yes."

"I have no more questions, your honor."

"Mr. Pollack, redirect?"

"Not, at this time, your Honor.

"You are excused, Mrs. Walker. Let's break for Lunch and reconvene at one o'clock. Be ready to call your next witness, Mr. Prosecutor."

Matthew took Susan to the EL Dorado Café for

lunch and was back at the courtroom fifteen minutes before one o'clock. Early enough, to see John be taken into the courtroom. "Matthew, my used-to-be friend. Come to try to put a nail in my coffin, are you?"

"Yes, John, I will have truth as my hammer. I will see you put away for a long time. This is not a threat but a promise."

"Talk, talk, talk, it means nothing to me." John's attorney is struggling to get him into the courtroom.

Susan is at Matthew's side and she starts to shake. "Matthew, he scares me. I do not trust him."

"I know, that's why we must do this. He belongs back in prison, with the key thrown away. Will you be okay, out here on the bench while I testify?"

"As far as I can tell, my sickness is done for the day. I will be fine, here." Matthew turns to go into the courtroom. "Matthew? Let me give you a kiss for good luck."

He stops with his hand on the doorknob. "Of course, what was I thinking?" He bends down for a peck on the cheek. Susan blushes. "You are so cute, you never used to blush, why are you shy, now?"

"I think I am feeling vulnerable with this pregnancy. I am surprised you noticed."

"Nothing about you, escapes my notice, my bride." She smiles at that, and blushes yet again.

Once on the witness stand, and sworn in, he gives his name, age and profession.

"Mr. Masters, did you or did you not, gamble away your father's farm fund?"

"Yes sir, not one of my proudest moments."

"Was it you that approached John for a scheme to get the money back?"

"No, he came to me and told me I can get the $200 dollars in one night doing a 'job'. I was desperate, John said he liked that in an accomplice."

"Were you at the Crap game on the Thursday before Anna went missing?"

"Yes, I was."

"What sort of behavior was John exhibiting that night?"

"He was very rude. He did not pick up my sister for their 'date'. Then he would not buy her a drink. He seemed focused on Anna the whole time. He bought Anna a drink, that she didn't ask for so Susan took it to try to diffuse the situation. But nothing helped. John was like a firecracker with a fuse that we could not put out."

"About the interrogation, what if anything, did you hear John say?"

"He wouldn't tell us anything until his cousin, insisted that his wording was a cover for the truth. He kept saying that he would not tell us anything which Susan said meant that he had information to tell. She got so mad at him, she kicked him hard, and broke his nose a second time. I was never so drawn to someone as I was when she did that."

"Give me a break!! That is disgusting, Matthew!"

"You were warned not to interrupt repeatedly, Mr. Walker. Bailiff, put Mr. Walker in a holding cell for the rest of the proceedings, today." John struggled but he was no match for the three bailiffs that came to remove him.

Matthew was only on the stand for a half an hour after that. He came out to Susan. "It wasn't as much fun without John in the room."

Susan just smiled. "You take pleasure out of the oddest situations, Matthew. I should be worried."

"I am the one to be worried, I just told the courtroom under oath that I was drawn to you when you kicked and broke John's nose a second time. I learned my lesson, don't ever piss off Susan Walker!" He says as he bends down and kisses her forehead.

"Well then, you can never say you weren't warned, husband. Let's get out of here."

SEVENTEEN

October 8ᵗʰ, 1866 Monday
An Excerpt from Elizabeth Lewis's Journal

I had to stop there, the other night. These are not pleasant memories to bring up. So much heartache. But there was heroism too. I must tell you of my young lady friend named Sally Young. She was out for an early morning ride with two suiters. As they entered back into town, they saw the columns of armed men and assumed that they were the Union Army. They heard the first shots fired and trotted past several victims, one of them being Reverend Snyder who was the Colonel in charge of the Negro Regiment. Sally now assumed the worst and told her suitors to ride quickly out of town. She said that she is going to help somehow. As she was on her way to the Eldridge Hotel where she was a seamstress, she was stopped and her pony was taken from her. As she argued with the ruffian in front of her, she came onto the plan that she would lead but mislead these bushwhackers as they tried to find those on Charlie Hart's Death List. Her offer to help was accepted. She took them on wild goose chases. Then when she had to get them to the person on the list, she fought for them to be spared. She claimed that they were related. Each was an Uncle, brother-in-law or cousin. The Rebels got tired of her 'help.' They told her that she was no longer needed but she tagged along, anyway, interceding where she could. After the Massacre, some family members who saw her with the outlaws had her arrested. At her trial, over a dozen people testified that she talked the Raiders out of killing them. I am so proud of her strength, and the commitment to make a difference. She could have been shot by the Raiders, when they realized that she was leading them astray, but she insisted on accompanying them at her own peril.

Another such story is the one that saved my father-in-law, Clyde Lewis. After he and my Uncle Daniel left, that morning of the Massacre, they went the long way around to get to town. Charlie's plan to infiltrate and take the town was perfect. He had so many men hit so many places at once that no one had a chance to organize or try to reach the armory for the town's weapons. Father Clyde and Uncle could tell that they were outnumbered and that it was hopeless from the start. Just after entering the downtown area, they found themselves surrounded by Raiders and it looked as if they were trapped. Uncle Daniel was very worried about his Gun shop, so Father Clyde suggested they split up. A decision that he regrets to this day.

Father Clyde heard that they were letting people take refuge at the City Hotel and he wanted to see if the boys were there. He got half-way there when he encountered a woman in a yard who called him over. She explained that the bushwhackers were shooting men indiscriminately and that he should take cover. He explained that he was looking for his grandsons who were at the encampment. She shook her head no. "It's too late for them. They were killed! All of them!! Please just hide, I can help, I've hidden five men already." Father Clyde did not know what to do. She just said that his grandsons were dead. He had to survive to get back to me and the kids and it was madness all around him.

He looked at the woman, "Who are you and how do you know the men will be safe?"

She smiled at him. "Who I am doesn't matter, but you are four feet from five men and you don't see them do you?"

Father Clyde looked around the open yard. There were tufts of wild grass growing in the summer heat but no structures within twenty feet. "I'm convinced. Hide me until this blows over, I must get back to my remaining grandchildren and their mother." As he said that he started crying as he took what he thought was a coward's way out, but he was a very big man and knew that he was not thinking straight with the deaths of his boys. Therefore, he'd be a big old slow target for any ruffian.

The woman walked to him, reached out and wiped his tears. "You'll be safe, hon, I promise." She walked two feet away and bent down and grabbed a handful of wild grass. It moved easily and under it was a door to a root cellar. She opened the door and told Father Clyde to get down. There were five men waiting in this dark place with a single lantern. Before the morning was over, five more men joined them. This unknown woman saved eleven men's lives, but not without peril to herself. The ninth man in the cellar was being followed by a Raider when he 'disappeared'. The woman was questioned but she refused to answer them. The Raider put his revolver to her temple and said, "Tell me or I will shoot you."

She looked at him, "You may shoot me, if you will, but you will still not find out where the man is." The Raider could tell that she would not tell him and he gave up and just left. No one knows who the woman was, she did not come back to let them out. After the shooting stopped, they ventured out on their own. No one ever saw her, again. Father Clyde said she was his guardian angel. I believe she was also!

Then there was Judge and Mrs. Riggs. Mr. Samuel Riggs was our District Attorney three years ago. He had the warrant for Charlie's arrest drawn up, so he was at the top of Charlie's Death list and a Ruffian on a horse cornered him in the front yard of his house. His wife ran out to stand with him. When the Raider went to shoot him, Samuel reached up and knocked the revolver and then ran away. As if it was communicated in advance, Mrs. Riggs grabbed the reins of the Bushwhackers horse and held on so that her husband could get away. She held on and got dragged about the yard and over their wood pile and back into the street. Samuel was still in sight and the rider took aim, again. Mrs. Riggs grabbed the other rein and turned the horse away from her husband's direction. Sarah Riggs suffered many hits to her head and arms with the butt of the Rebel's revolver while being dragged but her husband survived that day, thanks to her heroics.

EIGHTEEN

Sunday, October 10th, 1937
In Lawrence, Kansas

Anna and Henry are shopping after Service for a little dresser for the baby. Henry can recall the first time he took Anna into stores in EL Dorado. It was the Sunday after Matthew's 'job' and Henry was trying to see if there was any talk in town regarding the robbery. He remembers watching Anna, thinking how simple she was and that it was a bad thing that she was a homebody like her mother.

"How could I have been so wrong?" He says out loud in the second store they were in."

"Wrong about what, Henry? Don't you like this dresser? I think it's adorable." Anna says.

"No, honey, I was thinking of something else. This is a perfect little dresser for the spot we have. But it is priced a little high, let me see if I can get the price down by haggling."

"Henry, I would prefer you didn't. I get so embarrassed that it draws attention to the fact we cannot afford it."

"It doesn't hurt to ask. Even rich people haggle, Anna, that's how they got rich, not paying full price."

Henry is successful in knocking a few dollars off the price then asks Anna, "Where do you want to eat?"

"Henry, have you ever had a Pizza Pie?"

"No, what is that?"

"I cannot explain it but it's delish! There is an Italian restaurant just down the street from here. Let's go there, I am starving!!

They are seated in the darkened dining room and Henry says, "I cannot see the menu in this light. How is not seeing our food, romantic?"

"I never thought of it as romantic. But I was only here once." She thinks back to the days that she called herself Rosanne. "Joshua, brought me here before taking me to the movie, '*Show Boat.*'"

"You were on a date here with Joshua?" Henry can feel a sudden dislike of the restaurant. "You never mentioned that you actually dated him, Anna."

"I only agreed to go out with him, to let him down gently. He did not know that I miscarried and I needed to convince him that I was not good enough for him. He deserved better."

"How can you say that? There is nothing wrong with you, you are his equal in every way."

"Except for the fact that my heart belonged to someone else. He deserves to have someone love him like I knew I loved you, even if I did not remember you. It was very hard to convince him so I had to threaten to leave the Plantation if he did not stop trying to woo me. I do love him, like I love Carolyn and the Colonel. When I put it that way, I think he understood. He did not like it but he understood it. Anyway, I am starving! We had a pizza with sausage, peppers and onions. Doesn't that sound good?"

"Whatever you say, my darling. I am so glad that you fought for me. It was very brave of you to insist that I was out there. I would have not liked having to go up against Joshua for your feelings. He would have won hands down based on what he can give you against all the things I cannot."

"What you give me, money cannot buy. You make my heart smile!!" She reaches over to grab his hand and squeezes it. "And you gave me, a bun in the oven! What else can a girl want? Besides Pizza, where is our server? Don't they know they have a woman eating for two, starving to death over here!!

They thoroughly enjoy their pizza and before they leave, Henry asks, "Did you want to see a movie? We can go see what's playing, if you want."

"Ooh, I would love to, but I want to get home for the next excerpt of Beth's Journal. Whenever I think I have it difficult, I think of what she is going through. She is made of some tuff stuff!"

"So, are you Anna. No one else would have survived all that you have suffered and still had to the will to keep going."

NINETEEN

October 10th, 1866 Wednesday
An Excerpt from Elizabeth Lewis's Journal.

My William was reading my journal last night and said he thought my writing was an important thing to do. Our children need to know and their children need to know. If we don't remember the past, what's to keep us from repeating it? Isn't that the adage? He told me that he will get me two more journals so that I can add more stories of our neighbors.

What was odd about the whole ordeal is that most of those men on Charlie's Death List, managed to get away, while innocent, uninvolved men suffered greatly. It seems that the men who were naturally averse to the Southern cause (Union soldiers, free negroes, politicians, vocal abolitionist like John Speer the publisher) were the first to hide and live, while most men with no affiliation to either cause naively stood and died. Though there were a great number of guerrillas burning, and looting, they were not taking any personal chances. If they thought that someone might fight back, they abandoned them and went on to easier prey. So, many men ran into yards, fields and ravines and though they were shot at, hardly a Raider dare follow them into the fields, woods or the tall grasses for fear of being ambushed.

Newspaper Editor Josiah Trask was on the balcony of Dr. Jerome Griswold's house. He and his wife lived there with Harlow Baker and his wife (of the Ridenour & Baker Store) and State Senator Simeon Thorpe and his wife. The Guerrillas approached guns drawn and explained that they were going to BURN Lawrence to the ground and since they wanted to do it safely, they wanted the men under guard to prevent them from doing anything to stop them. The man on the balcony thought it sounded reasonable so they came out and were robbed immediately. They were lined up single file to march them to wait safely at central location but they did not get more than twenty feet away when all were shot down. Trask and Griswold died immediately. Thorpe and Baker lay wounded with the four wives trying to get to them. They posted a guard on the bodies. The two were in agony but did not move for hours. After a while attention was drawn to them and an order was given to shoot them again as they were abolitionists. They shot Baker again and the bullet went through his lung and out. Later a bushwhacker approached the bodies and ripped his pockets with a knife to rob him (though it was done before) but Baker did not make a sound or move a muscle. The four wives watched from their unburnt porch. After all the Raider left Lawrence, Thorpe was carried into the house but died the next day. Baker got up and walked with the aid of other survivors and despite all his wounds lived.

Mayor George Washington Collamore lived just a little past Doc Griswold. His son Hoffman was the first official casualty of the Massacre. He was up in the wee hours and was 'going-a-huntin'. The whole hoard happened upon him on the outskirts of town, before daylight and Hoffman must have assumed that this many men were Union troops this far into Kansas. Just a few words were exchanged before shots were fired on the lad. Both he and his pony were shot but they took off into a field. Hoffman got away from the Raiders and made it to a farmhouse. He died some hours later. He was only sixteen and a friend of my Ian. His father, the Mayor was on the Death List, he was warned by his wife to hide. He went down the well in a well-house along with their hired black man. The house was sacked and burned, the well-house caught on fire also and it is thought that the well's oxygen was sucked out to feed the fire and it suffocated both men in it. After the Massacre, the Mayor's friend Capt. Lowe climbed down the rope to retrieve the bodies but lost his footing and fell and died.

My poor friend, Getta Dix hid her children and maid in the coal shed far behind her house. The raiders looted her home after both her husband and his brother surrendered. She ran into the street and saw her young brother-in-law get shot, she sat down and put his head in her lap and wailed. When she saw her husband in custody being marched in the street, she started to rise and her brother-in-law's brain fell out into her hands. She dropped the bloody mess. She started to scream a heart breaking scream. and ran to her husband and clung to him and begged him to be safe. She turned to his captures, she was beside herself, crying and wailing but the leader of the band just said, "I am going to kill every damn one of them!" They pulled her away and shot all seven men in the alleyway, multiple times. The guerrillas rode away then turned around and kicked their horses hard to trample over the bodies. Getta stood rocking from the horror. After that she wandered up and down the street, getting in the way of other looters. She got back to her husband's body, she had found a straw hat along the way and she laid down next to his battered body, kissing him good-bye, she put the hat on his face to shield him from the morning sun. She then got up and calmly walked into her burning home, never to be seen again. She was one of the few women that were harmed in the Raid. All that she had seen undid her mind. The raiders drove her mad but her death was self-afflicted.

Newspaper publisher John Speer and his three sons were all on the List. John Jr. (nineteen) was shot by Larkin Skaggs at the newspaper office. Charles (seventeen) was working at another newspaper, and slept in the building as did a type-setter. The building was burned so badly that no bodies were found, but it was assumed they perished in the fire. John Sr. ran out of the back of the house into the cornfield when the Raiders rode up and yelled for him to surrender. Billy (fifteen) came out of the front of the house and when asked his name, he lied and said, "Billy Smith". The Raider's checked the List and saw no Billy Smith so they let him go. He did not get far when he decided to hide under a porch. He felt that would be worse for him if found and came out from under it, just in time to see some Ruffians dismount to burn a house. He offered to hold their horses. He held the reins while the house burned and the raiders thanked him by punching him about the head, for having a 'look' on his face. Afterward, Billy made it back home, just in time to get a rifle from his mom and shoot Larkin Skaggs, the last Raider left in the town who unbeknownst to him, had killed his oldest brother and who had just shot Nathan Stone.

TWENTY

Friday, October 15th, 1937
In EL Dorado, Kansas

Melinda and Mark Collins are at the District Attorney's Office at 8 a.m. just as Anna, Henry, Susan and Matthew were on the days they had to testify. Melinda was going to be the first on the stand. She was glad that her husband will not be allowed in the courtroom. Even though Mark knew of her relationship with Henry, she did not want it to embarrass him in the trial. Mark is her best friend as well as her husband. He waited, so patiently for Melinda to see him, the real him. He and Susan had organized a fund-raiser to buy Pa's new truck. He arranged with Grant Johnson, his distant cousin, to give the Masters free rent at the encampment and then offer Judd a foreman's job. He went out with Henry and Matthew looking for Anna's body. He held Melinda's hand, or wiped her tears or just stayed with her while she worked through the grief of losing her best friend and sister.

Melinda was devastated after John's confession. She felt so guilty for having wanted to be wild and leave the family. All Anna wanted was for things not to change. She wanted Melinda to fall in love and stay with them so they could have babies together. She and Anna talked about this several times. Melinda knew she hurt Anna's feelings when she talked about yearning to go out on her own. Then when Anna was taken, nothing else mattered but family. Family gets you by. Family sticks together. Family understands and loves you anyway. She had that kind of family and felt guilty that it took Anna's death to make her see them, in that way.

Now, it was time to testify against the evil man who ripped the hearts out of her family and out of Henry. She hopes that her testimony will be the one that sways the jury to put him in prison for good.

The District Attorney Anthony Pollack is warning Melinda about talking to directly, John, since so many of her family has done so already. "It really makes the

Defense Attorney, John and the Judge mad. We don't want the Judge mad at our side, believe me. He has kicked John out of the courtroom on three separate occasions. That makes the juries believe he has control issues. So, I want you to try to paint a picture of the uncontrollable John Walker, if you can."

"I will try, sir. Believe me I will try very hard."

Melinda is called in to testify and is sworn in. She is asked her name, age and profession. "My name is Mrs. Melinda Masters Collins. I am nineteen years old and I work as a cashier for the Kroger Grocery Store on Main St."

"Were you dating John Walker at the time of your sister's disappearance?"

"Yes and No. I let him take me to the Social at the Encampment then to the Crap Game that night. I went out with him one other night after that I think. I was supposed to be his date for the Crap Game on that Thursday but he never showed up to take me and he had to be forced by Susan to even consider buying me a drink. Then after the bouncers took him out, both his cousin Susan and I had to find our own rides home."

"Why were you dating him? Were you attracted to him?"

"I dated him because he asked me out. He wanted to be a big shot to me and take me to the crap games, so I let him. I always had my baby brother with me as a chaperone, though. I really did not trust John, but I could not put my finger on why."

"The night of the interrogation, it has been testified that you saved his life by stopping Henry from cutting his throat, is that true?"

"I should have let him do it. None of us would need to be here right now." She looks over to John for the first time, and smiles.

"Why did you stop Henry?"

"I thought I could get John to tell us where her body was. I begged him to tell us so we could give her a proper Christian Burial. I begged him not to let her rot exposed to the elements in the Kansas dirt, but he wouldn't or couldn't. I do not know which, but he didn't lead us in any direction that was the way he took her."

"Thank you Mrs. Collins, you've been very helpful."

Mr. Pollack turns and sits down.

The Defense Attorney gets up and walks to Melinda. "Mrs. Collins weren't you having relations with my client and Henry at the same time that Henry was having relations with Anna?"

"What? That whole sentence confused me. I never had relations with John. Like I said, my brother Matthew was my chaperone, every time I went out with John. What was the rest you asked?"

"Were you or were you not having relations with Henry while he was having relations with Anna?"

"No sir, Henry and I broke it off when he started to get more serious with Anna. He did not double-dip."

"Who's idea was it to break it off? Yours or Henry's?"

"Mine, I guess but he knew it was time. He realized we were having a fling but what he had with Anna was true love. Like what I have now with my husband, Mark. What does this have to do with John raping my sister? I do not understand this line of questioning."

"Your Honor, can you ask the witness not to ask me questions?"

"She has a point, counselor, what does this line of questioning have to do with the attack on her sister?" The Judge asks.

"Your Honor, John's head was manipulated by all these people using him for their sordid love triangles and they are all involved around his arch enemy Henry Harrick. I am trying to make the Jury see this."

"Flimsy defense but I will let you proceed. Any other questions for Mrs. Collins?"

"Yes sir, I am almost done. Mrs. Collins, you were at the Crap Game on the night of the punch. Correct?"

"Yes, I was there."

"Did you see Henry attack Mr. Walker with a sucker punch?"

"No, I did not. Anna and I were in the Ladies Room."

"Were you not a witness to various threats to John from Henry?"

"No, I was not."

"Were you aware that John was hoping that both the Masters girls were in that truck, that morning?"

Melinda starts to tremble. "Yes." She says just above a whisper.

"If you were in that truck, Anna wouldn't have been raped. He wanted to just scar the both of you but you weren't there so Anna had to get double. How does that make you feel?"

"I feel sick to my stomach and I am not pregnant. I have thought about this before you brought it up. Anna said that John said, he was disappointed that I was not there, also. How do you think I should feel with that kind of information? I am happy that I wasn't hurt, and I feel guilty that Anna got in all instead of me. But I am not on trial here." Melinda says with her face turned to the jurors. "John is the only guilty party here."

The Defense Attorney says. "Objection, your Honor, she has no right to make that declaration. I would like to have it stricken from the record."

The Judge looks to the Jurors. "Please disregard this witnesses opinion of John Walker, this is your job to decide."

"I have no more questions, your Honor."

"Mr. Pollack, any redirect?"

"Just one question for the witness, your Honor." He turns to Melinda. "Mrs. Collins, did you believe John Walker's confession."

Melinda takes a moment. The jury could hear her make a small whimper. She is looking down at her hands as she says in a low voice, "It cut through my heart, like I was stabbed." Then she looks up at the Jury just as her tears escaped her eyes. "I believed he thought that he did what he set out to do. He set out to take the one thing that Henry loved the most. I believe that he believed he had killed her."

"Thank you, Melinda." Mr. Pollack turns to the Judge. "I have no more questions, for this witness, your Honor."

"Thank you for your testimony, Mrs. Collins, you may step down. I think it is time for a short break, be back in your places in fifteen minutes." The gavel strikes.

Melinda leaves the witness stand and exits the courtroom. Mark is waiting on the bench outside. Melinda walks straight to Mark's shoulder and buries her head in it. "It was harder than I imagined." She starts to cry. "Mark, I am so sorry. I wish I could take back everything that I did before I knew you. What I did with Henry, how I lied to Anna, every day for a month, and especially getting involved with John. I know he is the guilty one but that doesn't lessen the gravity of my mistakes." He puts his arms around her and hugs her tightly.

"We've all made mistakes, Melinda. Yours are no worse than mine." He kisses the top of her head. "The fact that you recognize them as mistakes, is the thing that makes it all better, now"

She looks up at her husband. "I cannot think of a single mistake that you have made, Mark. You have always been good." She puts her head back against his shoulder.

"Melinda, if I had the guts to ask you out, before Henry or John, none of this might be happening, either. Did you ever think of that? I met you before the Harrick's moved into the encampment and before you started picking in the fields. I fell for you the moment I saw you, but couldn't bring myself to tell you. This can all be my fault!"

Melinda looks up at her husband in disbelief and confusion. "Say that again?"

They are interrupted with the bailiff coming out of the courtroom and calling Mark for his testimony.

Mark enters the courtroom without another word and leaves her standing there shocked by his admission. His testimony goes smoothly. He is just asked about the search and interrogation. He is on the stand for less than a half an hour. When he exits, Melinda is waiting for him with a smile on her face.

She walks up to him and takes his face in her hands and kisses him sweetly. "Mr. Mark Collins, I love you so much." Mark just blushes.

Mr. Pollack is very pleased with the day's witnesses.

TWENTY-ONE

October 15th, 1866, Monday
An excerpt from Elizabeth Lewis's Journal.

After discussing it at length with my William, I think I am ready to tell the tale of how my baby died. I last told you that Charlie Hart, (William Quantrill), had given the mid-wives Laudanum for me. After I drank it, I was barely aware of the labor pains or her delivery. She came out alive but barely breathing. She was starting to get blue from lack of oxygen. Mrs. Caldwell was holding her and trying to clear her airway. My Lizzie was getting very upset. She started crying which started Willie to cry. I was in and out of it, but I called to Lizzie to get help.

My poor little Lizzie took Willie and ran out of the room. Her idea of help was to call the one person who seemed to be the one in control, she went out looking for Charlie Hart. Quantrill was out of the Hotel and on the way, out of town. She saw our buckboard, with my dead father still on the bed board, and she climbed up in the seat with Willie and took off. She headed toward the City Hotel, because she heard Charlie talk about how he thought Mr. Nathan Stone was the only other person in town that he liked. She drove the buckboard with great speed (considering this was her first time at the reins). She found a large group of Raiders, waiting for their leader to say good-bye to his long-time friend. She had the presence of mind to ask for William Quantrill, telling the Raiders that he was her uncle and that she needed him. Though they laughed at her, they decided to see that she get to him. Imagine his surprise when they brought her and Willie to him and announced that they were his niece and nephew.

Charlie smiled at them. "Lizzie, my dear, what may I do for you?" He got off his horse and came to the buckboard to talk with her.

"Mr. Quantrill, you need to help my Ma, she had the baby but the baby is dying. Please, do something, please." She must have been very convincing because Charlie got into the buckboard and came back to the

Hotel with Jesse James and a tall man, following on horseback, and leading his horse.

Charlie knocked on the room door and had Lizzie come in first. She looked around and saw that the baby was still blue.

"Please Mr. Quantrill . . . hurry," she called out.

He came into the room, and crossed over to the baby in Mrs. Caldwell's arms. She reluctantly, let him take her from her. I was yelling, no, but I was yelling it in my mind, only. I was not saying anything, out loud. I was still not in control of my body.

He calmly took the struggling newborn, sat down and un-swaddled her. He placed her chest side down on his knee, carefully holding her head. He patted her back, patting harder and faster. Clara had not cried since she was born but his patting got her to cry. As she cried harder, her color came back. He stopped and turned her over and brought her to his shoulder. "There, there now, you're going to be just fine. Mrs. Lewis, did you have a name for this fine little girl?"

I barely managed to say that her name is Clara, before I lost consciousness again. I am told that he held her for quite a few minutes. She cried a very healthy cry the whole time. He crossed the room and gave her to her older sister, Lizzie. Lizzie smiled and thanked him and even with the crying baby in her hands, my ten-year-old hugged him, tight around the waist. I am told that Charlie got a little emotional at this.

William Quantrill, got his emotions in check and straightened up. He told Lizzie that she was a very brave little lady. Clara quieted down in Lizzie's arms and she held her as she followed Charlie out of the room, and down the stairs. As Charlie left the Hotel, Lizzie followed him out the Front door, well, almost.

Her way was barred by the very tall Raider that had come back with Charlie. "Just a moment, little girl." Said Bill Anderson, known as 'Bloody Bill'. "I think we've had just about enough out of you."

Lizzie opened her mouth to explain that she wanted to say good-bye to Colonel Quantrill but Anderson reached out and grabbed Clara from her arms. "That's my new sister, Colonel Quantrill just saved her life!" She said.

"Well, he might have done that, but you have put our Leader in peril. We are late in leaving this town and it is your fault! I am going to punish you." He raised his one arm to hit Lizzie when Jesse James called out to him.

"Come on Bill, leave the ladies alone. Colonel needs to get on the road, right?" Jesse asked. He was standing in the doorway, behind Anderson.

Anderson said in a very small voice, to Lizzie, "Can you catch?" He was about two feet from her as he said this and he, suddenly, threw the baby over her head. The baby landed on the wood floor of the Hotel entranceway.

Lizzie ran to her. Clara looked as if she was sleeping. Lizzie held her tight, and looked up at Anderson. "How could you do that to a baby?" She asked.

"You should ask Major Ewing how he could have killed my one sister and crippled the other. I think this makes us almost even." He started to cross the gap between them but Lizzie backed away.

Jesse James put a hand on his arm. "Bill, the Colonel will not like this. We need to get going. Come on, now!" He tugged even harder on Anderson's arm and Anderson finally turned around and walked out without another word. Jesse James said to Lizzie, "Go back to your mother, Lizzie. Sorry about Bloody Bill." With that he followed Bill out and closed the Hotel door behind him.

Lizzie came back up the stairs. She handed the baby to Mrs. Caldwell. Mrs. Caldwell began to wrap her up again but she saw that Clara was not breathing. "What happened, she was fine?" She turned her over like Charlie did and patted her, and patted her, and patted her. Clara would not cry, she would not wake up, she was gone. When Bloody Bill Anderson tossed Clara, she broke her neck when she landed on the floor. She died immediately but Lizzie did not know!

I had come to as my Lizzie was lying next to me crying and saying she was sorry. She was saying that it was her fault that little Clara was dead. I did not understand. I saw Charlie save Clara's life. He was here because Lizzie got him to come back. That act of hers saved Clara's life. How could she be dead? I struggled to get out of bed to see the baby myself. Miss Petrie stopped me and sat me down and told me what Bloody Bill Anderson did.

I went back to the bed and to my brave little Lizzie and held her and told her she was not to blame. I told her that I loved her and could not be more proud of how she handled herself today.

I was trying to be brave, myself. My Father was dead. My baby was dead. I did not know where my boys were, or if they were dead. I did not know where my Uncle or Father-in-law or my William were. But I had my Little Lizzie and my young Willie and I held onto both and thank God out loud for my blessings.

Lizzie looked at me, "How can you thank God, Mama, your baby is dead?" I heard Mrs. Caldwell gasp.

"I thank God that I have both of you safe in my arms and that GOD has our Clara safe in his. Lizzie, I believe that with all my heart. Clara is with God AND Papa. No harm will ever come to them again. And I think it is time we went home."

Mrs. Caldwell and Miss Petrie told me that it was too soon for me to travel. They told me I could bleed to death, riding in a buckboard all the way home. I had to be strong, and I had to get home. I had to prepare my father and my daughter Clara for burial. I had to see if any of the men in the family would come home to me. It was all I could do now - wait.

Mrs. Caldwell insisted on coming with me. She was about fifty years old and a very stout woman. She practically lifted me into the bed of the buckboard next to my dead father. I rode laying down with my poor cold Clara in my arms as she let Lizzie drive. It let Lizzie feel in control of an otherwise uncontrollable situation. I don't know how I would have managed without Mrs. Caldwell.

TWENTY-TWO

Saturday, October 16th, 1937
In Lawrence, Kansas

Anna did not like Beth's entry last night. She clutched her belly protectively during the whole telling. Henry was sitting on the sofa with her and he could tell that it was bothering her.

Carolyn got very upset, also. She cried and hugged her grandfather. The Colonel has stayed engaged during the readings. He said he remembers coming home on the buckboard with his dead Papa, his Mother and his dead sister, with his sister Lizzie driving.

Joshua and Henry have finally finished harvesting the sunflower heads and Henry has spent the last two days tilling under the acreage. Very tiring work, even on a new farm tractor. Henry loved the feel of the tractor's power under him. He can recall Anna saying that she wanted to live on a farm and have a side garden like her Ma. So, true to her word, even though she did not know her identity, she had Carolyn's foreman till up a patch on the side of the Main house. She planted all the fruit, vegetables, and flowers that her mom had and more. He told her back then that he never wanted this kind of life. He was so wrong!! This is the best life there is. Good hard work for great people. Having them love Anna as much as he does. Going into the Main house anytime he wants just to see her smile so he can feel it in his heart! I am so very blessed! He thinks as the tractor hums under him.

Today is Henry's off day but he still had a part of the field left. He did not like leaving things unfinished. The early afternoon was a cool one. He thought that the day would have warmed up by now. He was in a hurry to finish. He wanted to get back to his little home where Anna was crocheting baby booties. She has been in a phase where she wants to make all sorts of goodies for the babe. She has made two baby blankets out of the softest yarn he has ever felt and next she will make some baby caps for the little one. He or she will be born before the Holidays but that means he or she will only know months of cold drafty days in their little home, and cold rides to the Main House. So, caps, booties and blankets will come in very useful. Anna is so smart about these things.

As Henry was lost in thought, Joshua comes into the field wildly waving his arms to stop Henry. Henry immediately brings the tractor around to get to Joshua. *God, don't let this be about the baby*, he thinks.

"Henry, you must come to the house, we have Dr. Mason on the way already. The Colonel found your Da on the floor in the sitting Room. You go to the Main House. I will go get Anna for you."

Henry drives the tractor straight to there. He bursts through the front door. He is met by Carolyn. "Henry, he was asking for you." They walk into the sitting Room where Da is on the couch. Carolyn follows him and explains. "He was here attending the Colonel and after stoking the fire he just went down, according, to my grandfather."

"Da, what's happened? Are you having pain? Is it your heart?" Henry looks at his father's face. It is drooping on one side.

He can see his father struggling to talk. He is only gurgling out sounds, none of them sound like words. "Oh, Da, I think you are having a stroke!" He turns to Carolyn, "Joshua said Dr. Mason is on the way?" She nods. He turns back to his father. "Da, I am here, I will not leave your side. Help is on the way and Anna will be here soon. Just lie there, don't try to talk any more. Try to relax." He turns back to Carolyn. "I wonder if his blood pressure has been high, recently. He takes it himself but he never tells us what it is. How long ago did you call Dr. Mason?"

"About twenty minutes ago. I was just coming down the stairs when I heard him collapse. The Colonel started ringing his bell wildly and yelling. I got here first but Joshua was right behind me. Together, we got him on the couch. Then we called for the doctor and then to the little house to get you. Anna told us that you had gone to till the last of the sunflower field so Joshua went to get you then Anna."

Henry continued to hold Da's hand while Carolyn goes to get a wet towel for Da's brow. A few minutes later, Anna comes rushing in. "Henry, where's Da? She asks as she is rounding the corner into the sitting room. "Henry, how is he?" As she says this she too notices the drooping side of the face. She lowers herself to Da and gives him a kiss on his forehead. "Don't you worry, Da, Dr. Mason will be here very shortly."

Frank Harrick can only look up and mumble something unintelligible. He tries to give her a weak smile. "Da are you in pain?" She asks. He mumbles again. "Da we cannot understand you right now. If you are in pain, close your eyes." He opens them wide. "Good, so no pain. Close your eyes if you'd like a glass of water." He closes them. Carolyn hurries to get him a glass. "Da, did you pass out? Close your eyes for yes." He closes them again. "Were, you dizzy first? He opens wide his eyes. "So, he was not dizzy." Carolyn brings him water and a straw. Anna puts the straw in the side of the mouth that is not drooping but as he drinks, the droopy side is leaking slightly.

Finally, after ten more minutes, Dr. Mason is at the house with an ambulance. He pulls Henry to the side and asks, "Is this his first stroke that you know about?"

"Yes doc, I think so. How serious is this, will he die from this?"

"Well, Henry, the damage you see is done. We will stabilize him and . . . he might have permanent disability or it might be temporary. It's too soon to tell." Frank's blood pressure is 205 over 95 when the medics take it. "We have the culprit right here. Has he been taking his blood pressure pills?"

Anna interrupts. "I give Da his pills every morning. But I do not know what his pressure runs, regularly, either." Her eyes tear up. "I should have been more diligent."

Dr. Mason looks at his favorite patient. "It will be okay, Anna. Don't get yourself and the babe upset. I will personally take good care of Frank." As he is saying this, the orderlies are loading Da into the ambulance. "You can follow me to the hospital. We will have him in intensive care for a few hours, so do not hurry to get there."

Carolyn looks at Anna and Henry, after the ambulance carries Da away. "Looks like you both need a distraction for a while. Let's see what Gram Beth is writing about tonight." She smiles and they all nod in agreement and sit down for the next excerpt.

TWENTY-THREE

October 16^h, 1866 Tuesday
An Excerpt from Elizabeth Lewis's Journal

We have finally finished the Sunflower seeds and have delivered them all to the Sweet Shop. It is great to have such a large job finished. I could not have gotten it all done without my ladies' help. I negotiated a new price for these treats and after paying the harvest crew and my Ladies, we shall make a tidy profit! I think we should double our Sunflower crop next year. William and I need to discuss this thoroughly. He considers this crop a luxury and cannot see the future in it, like I do.

I had to take some time away from the writing, anyway. It hurt reliving it. Yet, the telling of the loss of my little one seemed to have lifted a weight off me. If I had not gone into town that day, my father and my baby both might be alive. I have carried that guilt in my heart for all these years. I had to assure Lizzie that she was blameless, but I have not been able to forgive myself. I have talked with Reverend Cordley on the matter many times and never felt as relieved of the guilt as putting the events down in this silly little journal.

I think that I would like to tell you more about the other townspeople. Reverend Richard Cordley, that I just referred to, is our Pastor at the Plymouth Congregational Church. He, his wife, child and a friend walked calmly through the streets until they reached tall reeds at the river's edge. An old friend on the opposite bank saw him and bravely rowed a skiff over and rescued them. It was a miracle, he insists because he was one of the only preachers on the Death List, that managed to go unmolested. His home, though paid the price. All that was left of it was "a bed of embers and ashes," as he puts it.

Sometimes it was the Raiders themselves that saved others. Cole Younger (now of the James-Younger Gang) touted responsibility for many deaths but he saved lives on at least two occasions. One man he found hiding in the closet in his nightshirt. When he pulled him out, his wife said, "Don't kill him, he has asthma so bad that he hasn't slept in bed for years." To which Cole Younger responded, "I do not kill men with asthma." Then he left. One house he entered with three other raiders and found three very elderly gentlemen. Though his partners were ready to shoot, Cole Younger made them leave, then he posted a guard at the door so that no other raiders would get to them.

Another story about Cole Younger is that he is an active member of the Free-Masons. He would display their secret hand signs upon encountering men. If they gave the countersign, he would bi-pass them and go off to find other possible victims. Dozens of men claimed to have been saved through this method, with Cole Younger.

A young Billy Bullene, only about ten or eleven at the time, had seen nine men shot. He helped several men to escape. The Union Army Recruiting Office was across the street of his home. The officer on duty was trapped inside in uniform when the Raiders were brandishing torches to burn the building to the ground. The officer stripped to his skivvies and ran across to the Bullene home and Billy gave him women's clothes to wear.

My William's good friend, John Bergen saved himself after being shot with six others, by lying under the corpses of two men and a fifteen-year-old boy, named Jim Pickens. When Mrs. Pickens, the mother, came to get his body for burial, Bergen pleaded with her to let the boy stay to protect him. She agreed and when the Massacre was over, John brought Jim's body to her and helped with his burial.

Mr. Winchell ran into the home of Union Army Chaplain, Dr. Charles Reynolds. He was away with the troops but his wife and two women friends were at home. Thinking fast, they shaved off Mr. Winchell's beard and put a tight bonnet on his head and put him in a disabled chair with lots of medicine bottles surrounding him. They even put white powder on his face to make him look sickly. They called him Auntie Betsie and fooled each of the Raiders that entered the house and none of them tried to burn the house down.

I must include my Uncle as one of the heroes. After he separated from Father Clyde, he made his way to his Gun shop. It was a small shop at the end of the business district. When he got there, it was still intact. He saw his friend Levi Gates cowering between buildings. He saw Uncle and looked around before running to him. He asked if he could hide in the shop, he had run out the back door of his house without having anywhere to run. The two men entered his shop and locked the door and they waited. Just a few moments went by when two women, knocked on the door, looking for their husbands. Uncle left Levi at the store, and with his rifle in hand, and guns in his belt, went out to help look. They crossed the street and saw a young boy protecting an old man's body in an alleyway. My uncle helped carry the man into the house for his wife to attend to him. He still had to look for his own nephews and the ladies' husbands so he was in the streets again.

Walking toward him was a Raider. He was swaying from drink. Uncle tried to dodge into a gangway but it had two other ruffians in it, already. One of the wives ran over to Uncle and tried to pretend that he was her husband and whispered to him, "Georgia just found her Bob and is trying to get him hidden, please stall, if you can." I am told that my Uncle told the Guerillas that this lady was a stranger to him, but he had a few friends in the chambers of his rifle and guns that he'd like them all to meet. They backed away a pace or two, when Levi poked his head out of the Shop and called to Uncle.

"Mr. Palmer, everything okay, there?" This made the men turn around and they must have seen the sign over the doorway that read, 'Daniel W. Palmer, Gunsmith'. While their attention was distracted, Uncle was able to kill one of them and shoot the other in the hip. The woman ran to the back of the house to hide. The injured Raider returned fire, hitting Uncle in the arm. Uncle ran to the shop and Levi locked the door.

The Raider called out to his comrades, "Quantrill's Raiders!! We must get Daniel W. Palmer, before we leave this town!!" Within a few seconds, the street had six men, all guns drawn, all aimed at the large window of the Gun Shop. Most of them were very drunk but they came at Uncle en masse. Uncle told Levi to get out the back, but Levi grabbed a gun and started loading it. As the mob was approaching, Uncle and Levi started shooting breaking the glass window. Two Ruffians were hit, but they still walked forward and were joined by three more men. Two Raiders were hit then went down, but now it was time to reload and though Uncle was very fast, Levi was not, and he got hit by a bullet. Uncle picked off one more, before the Raiders climbed into the window and shot him again. They tied Uncle to Levi and then to a post. They grabbed all the guns Uncle had on hand then they set fire to the shop. The back of the shop was engulfed in flames, but somehow they managed to untie themselves and jumped out the window only to be picked up by the bushwhackers and thrown back into the flames. As they did this, they congratulated themselves. A cry was heard over their shouts, "All Merciful God! Oh, God - Save Us!" Then just screams of agony. This made the Raiders cheer louder then they mounted their horses and rode away, laughing. My poor brave Uncle was gone but he and Levi killed three men and injured three more. The wives from across the street watched the whole thing, horrified.

TWENTY-FOUR

Sunday, October 17th, 1937
In Lawrence, Kansas

Yesterday, after hearing Beth's sad journal entry, Henry and Anna left to see if Da was doing any better. The Colonel said that he did not know that his great-uncle died that way. He said his mother hid all the horror from them when she could.

On the way to the Hospital, Henry says, "Da would have liked Uncle Daniel, he was a fighter until the end. Remind me to tell him about him or read that chapter to him later."

"Henry, did you notice Da's face?"

"Yes, I hope that is not permanent. The part that worries me is his speech. I think he thought he was saying real words." Henry looks over to Anna. She was holding back tears, he could tell. He reaches across to her. "Da is made of pretty strong stuff, I still think he will be able to bounce our little one on his knee. Don't worry, Anna."

They were ushered directly to Dr. Mason's office when they asked where Da was. Anna looked white with worry. "Henry, why would they not let us see him?" Anna asks.

"I am not sure, Anna, say a prayer that it is just their procedure after a stroke."

They wait some tense ten minutes, before Dr. Mason comes into the room. "Sorry to keep you away from your father. We have lots of tubes going to him and he is doing better that he looks. His stroke is serious, but I do not think he sustained any permanent damage. We just got him stable and we are removing some of the tubing so that you can see him."

Anna goes to the physician, "Thank you so much Dr. Mason." She gives him a kiss on the cheek. "We all owe you so much!" He blushes.

"You can go see him, I'll take you."

Frank did not try to say much, last night. He was conscience and alert and responded to their questions, with the eye blinking code.

This morning, Henry and Anna went to the early Service and asked Pastor Jonas to say an extra prayer for Da. They went straight to the Hospital, afterward.

Da was sitting up in bed, when they came to his room. He said, "Sorry to have given you both such a scare, yesterday." His speech still had a slight slur to it. "Anna please forgive me, and sit down. I hate seeing you standing up."

"Oh, Da, I am so relieved that you are better. I kept telling my babe that he had to talk with the man upstairs so that you will be around to bounce him or her. I knew that would work."

The food tray came in for Frank. Anna fussed over him and opened the containers for him. He went to grab a fork and they both saw his crumpled hand. It was unable to grasp the fork. Anna took his hand and tried to unclench it. She looks up at Henry but says to Da, "Am I hurting you by doing this?"

"No honey, it doesn't hurt but I do not think I can do this. Can you feed me? Please?" He pleads.

"Of course, Da, absolutely. It will give me practice for the babe." She says making light of the situation.

They spend most of the afternoon with Da, until Carolyn and Joshua show up. Anna and Henry let them visit for a bit, while they go grab something to eat. They go to the Hospital cafeteria for a quick bite. Henry looks at his glowing wife looking over the menu. She is chatting over the limited selection. "Why can't they have just a few more dishes! I could make it much better.

"Anna, would want to run a restaurant or own one someday?" She looks up strangely at her husband, with her mouth wide open. "Why are you looking at me that way?"

"Because I was just thinking that for the first time. I have so many ideas for a little hometown type place. Like Sally's Diner, I suppose. How did you know?"

"Well, I don't read minds but I could see you working it out as you were looking at the menu. I am thrilled that you know how to cook so well. It would be a shame that you don't delight more people with your dishes."

"I am looking forward to motherhood, first. I want several babies. When I get them off to school I will seriously consider starting a business. You would support me in this endeavor?"

"I would, I will be the dish washer for you. I like a long-term plan like this. We need to start saving for the restaurant."

"I figured if Great Gram Beth could run a laundry business with 4 babies, why couldn't I run my own place?" She looks down at her belly. "Right little one? Would you be proud if your mama was a business woman? *He* is kicking me. Do you think that's in agreement? Or that *she* doesn't like it?"

"The next question would be in EL Dorado or in Lawrence? I would assume you would not be taking care of the Colonel and running a restaurant."

"Yes, that would be difficult. Of course, we are looking at ten years from now. The Colonel would be in his Eighties by then so . . . Are we really talking about this?"

"It's just talk, until it isn't. In the meantime, we need to order food and get back upstairs. I don't want to leave Carolyn and Joshua up there too long."

"Henry, would you mind if I go home with them? I am so exhausted. This babe is wearing me out, plus with worrying about Da, it is too much of a strain."

"Of course Anna. I am so selfish. Please go home with Carolyn and Joshua."

Anna reaches over to grab his hand. "You do not have selfish bone in your body, my Henry!"

Anna goes straight to the Main house even though Joshua offered to take her to the Little house directly. "Anna, I thought you were exhausted?" He asks. "Why are you pushing it, when you could have a relaxing evening in your own quiet home?"

"I just wanted to see the Colonel. I haven't been very attentive to him and I feel guilty about it. I know you and Carolyn and even the Colonel himself have been limiting my being with him. I know that you think you are protecting me but you are not taking into consideration that I love the Colonel and I like taking care of him." Anna starts to tear up.

"Anna, we are not trying to keep you from him, we are just helping lessen the physical stress that his care can cause." Carolyn explains. "Come, tonight is another Journal entry." She leads them into the sitting room where the Colonel is snug in his chair but awake.

"The entries have been so depressing, lately. I am going to make a large pot of hot cocoa, for us. I know that will make it better. Colonel, do you want hot tea, instead?" Anna asks.

"No, Rosanne. Hot cocoa sounds great. How is Frank? I think about all the people that I have outlived and I am beginning to think that I don't like it."

"Frank is looking almost back to normal. He is still slurring a bit but a few more days he should be back to normal." Carolyn answers for Anna.

Anna heads to the kitchen and starts the cocoa. When it is finished, she starts to put the pot of cocoa and four tea cups on a tray and as she lifts it, she feels a strain in her womb. She lets go of the tray suddenly and the tea cups all clatter together covering up the sound of her moan. It does not matter, both Joshua and Carolyn run into the kitchen. They see Anna clutching her belly.

Carolyn runs to her. "Anna, what is it? Were you trying to carry that heavy tray? Come sit down." She leads her to one of the stools around the large marble island that is their kitchen table.

Anna is shaking. "Carolyn, I think something is wrong. Can you take me back to the hospital?" She says in a whisper. "I need to go to the bathroom. I feel something leaking!" She gets up and uses the one attached to the kitchen. Joshua pulls his car back up to the back door so Carolyn can take Anna back to the Hospital. He will stay with the Colonel.

Anna comes out of the bathroom. "I am bleeding. Let's hurry." Joshua has gotten her coat and is putting it around her shoulders. "Joshua, please call the hospital and make sure Henry stays there for me. The Cocoa is still hot, make sure the Colonel gets some, okay?"

"Anna do not worry about us. Go, please or I will call you an ambulance! Let me help you to the car."

Carolyn is driving very carefully but with as much speed as she thinks is possible. Anna is beside her breathing funny, can she be going into labor? She is only at seven months. Can the baby live that young if born alive? These thoughts, are all running through her mind. Poor Henry, he will have his father and his wife hospitalized. She was in sort of the same position last year. Her grandfather was in with kidney stones while Anna had reinjured her neck. She was so torn with worry. She looks over at Anna, again. She is still panting. "Anna are you in pain?"

"I am feeling a heaviness between my legs. I do not like this." Anna goes back to panting.

Carolyn puts her hand on Anna's arm. "It will be okay, Anna."

Anna turns to her with tears in her eyes. "Promise Carolyn?" Carolyn nods but remains silent, holding back her own tears.

She pulls up to the front of the Hospital and Dr. Mason and Henry run out to meet the car. Henry opens the car door and picks up the love of his life. "Anna, I leave you alone for a few minutes and you go to this extreme to get my attention. It's not necessary. All you had to do was tell me to come home and I would have been at your side." She buries her head into his neck, crying.

"I am so scared, Henry. This is what it felt like when I lost our little girl. Why, why?"

"Dr. Mason is here, Anna. Let him do his magic, it'll be okay, I promise." He kisses her forehead as he puts her down on a hospital gurney that Dr. Mason has waiting for her.

"Henry, please wait here. Let us see what's going on. I will come for you as soon as I can. Promise." The doctor and nurses push Anna's gurney down the hallway then turn right at the next hallway.

Henry is left standing there. He did not have a chance to say good-bye or good-luck. He starts running his hand through his hair. Carolyn has parked Joshua's car and is now beside Henry. She reaches out for his hand. He takes it and kisses the back of it. "You have been like a sister to her, it can't be for nothing. She is going to be alright. The baby is going to be alright. I know it. My whole life is in danger and it HAS to be alright!" He is crying. "I cannot live without her. I have tried doing that already. I cannot do it again."

"Henry, it won't come to that. She is a healthy

woman, now. The baby has been very healthy. There is no reason to go to that extreme. She is most likely just having preterm labor. It is a common occurrence, though can seem frightening at first." She is patting his hand now. "The only thing I can think of, is that we were going to read Gram Beth tonight and she did not want to hear it without you." She sees him smile.

"That would be my Anna." They wait together in the lonely lobby for hours with Henry pacing the hall and stopping to look at his watch, often. At one point, he says to Carolyn. "Looks like we will be a day late for that reading. It is five minutes to Oct 18th."

TWENTY-FIVE

Monday, October 18th, 1937
In Lawrence, Kansas

It is at two in the morning when Dr. Mason comes to get Henry and Carolyn. "I am sorry my dear boy. I didn't want to leave Anna's side until she and her babe were safe. Come, you can see her now. She was very brave and had a very hard time. It was touch and go for a while, I must tell you. I think the first miscarriage damaged her womb in some way and I do not know if she will survive another pregnancy. She is stable now and . . ." The Doctor trails off because he has opened the door to Anna's room and he sees Henry's eyes meet Anna's. There is nothing more he needs to say.

Henry was racked with worry about his wife. He imagined coming to see her dead or near death from the ordeal that she has been through this whole night. What he sees though, is his Anna with her hair all wavy as if fresh from a shower. She looks like an angel and she is sitting up and smiling down at the babe in her arms. "Henry, I'd like you to meet our Daughter. She is very, very tiny but Dr. Mason says she is healthy."

Henry rushes to her side. "Oh, Anna, the longer I waited, the surer I was that you were not going to survive. I am so sorry for doubting you. You are the most . . . God, I love you so much. Was it very bad for you?" He is kneeling at her bedside and stroking her beautiful wavy hair that falls just at her shoulders.

"It was at the beginning but they gave me something to stop the pain. I was so afraid to deliver so early. I thought I would bury another baby next to our first. I kept asking Doc if he could give me something to hold her in place. He told me to let go and trust that the Lord is guiding his hands. When I 'let go' as he put it, everything went smoothly. Look at her, Henry. She is perfect!"

Henry kisses Anna's cheek. "You are perfect! We haven't talked about names. What do you want to call her?"

"I am not sure. Do you want to hold her?"

"Anna, she is so tiny. I might break her." A small laugh comes from behind Henry. He forgot Carolyn was with him. "Carolyn, I am sorry, I forgot that . . ." He blushes. "Look at what Anna did. My perfect wife gave me a perfect daughter."

Carolyn comes a little closer. Henry and Anna can see she was crying happy tears, too. "Congratulations, both of you. Henry, your little girl will not break if you hold her. I am certain of that"

Henry reaches for his new baby. "She is so light. How much does she weigh? Did they tell you?"

"Four pounds, five ounces. She is not even a sack of flour!! Henry, would you like to call her Clara Beth? It would be after the Colonel's sister and his mother? I have always liked both of those names and they sound nice together."

Henry has not stopped looking at the babe in his arms. "Clara Beth is beautiful, Anna. She is just beautiful. I am such a lucky man!"

Carolyn is beside him. "Henry, Anna, you do not need to name her for some people you are not related to, just because we are reading a journal."

Henry looks at Carolyn, strangely. "Carolyn, we are related to you and the Colonel in everything but blood. Do not let me hear you say anything like that again. You and Joshua are siblings to my Anna and the Colonel is her grandfather as much as he is yours. You adopted her by saving her life and we are eternally grateful. Now do you want to hold your niece Clara Beth, or don't you." He hands the baby to her and looks at his angel in the bed. She is smiling and tears are falling non-stop.

"Henry, I have never loved you more than I do right now!" She manages to say between sobs. She holds out her arms to him and he sits on her bed and wraps his arms around her. They kiss softly, sweetly and lovingly. Carolyn is rocking the little one and humming a lullaby. Anna says, "Life is perfect, Henry. Just as it should be. I love you so much!" She says this as Henry says "I love you so much". Then they both say, "Jinx, Double Jinx!" They all are laughing.

"I am being selfish, Anna. We need to call your family! They will want to be here. I would have called them from the lobby but I did not want them to share in my worry. I better go do it now! Carolyn, do you know where a pay phone is?'

Just then Dr. Mason walks in. "You can use the phone in my office."

Anna says, "But Doctor, we are calling long distance to EL Dorado."

"Anna, you are my favorite patient and I feel like you are a daughter to me. Henry call your in-laws, my treat! What are we going to name this perfect child?"

"Clara Beth." Carolyn, Henry and Anna say at the same time. "Jinx, Triple Jinx!" The Doctor just shakes his head at them as they are laughing.

"Carolyn, why don't we let the babe and the new Mother rest for a few hours. Go with Henry to make some calls and both of you take a nap in my office. I have two long couches in there that have been my bed many a night. This has been a long night for all of us."

Carolyn reluctantly puts Clara in the bassinette on the side of Anna's hospital bed. She looks up at the doctor. "Hey Doc, we were debating on when a baby can sit up and take solid food, how old would Clara be before she can to do that?"

"Being she is so tiny, her development will always be a little off so she will be about six to eight months old, before she has good control of her neck and able to sit up in a high chair. Why do you ask?"

"We found a high chair in my attic and it brought up a discussion among us as to how soon it should be before it comes out of the attic. Henry was right about the age. So, he wins."

"Carolyn, I am the winner of the million-dollar jack pot, today!" He says as he is still staring at his wife and child.

"Well, come on, DADDY, time to let your two perfections rest for a few hours." Carolyn turns him toward the doorway. "Who do you want to call first?" She is asking as they are leaving the room.

"You can call Joshua and the Colonel, I am going to Da's room and tell him that he is a Grandpa. Then I will call Mark's house to tell Judd and Judy. The thought of sleep is the farthest from my mind right now.

Henry sneaks into Da's room on the third floor. He

bends over his sleeping father. "Da, wake up, I must tell you something." Da's eyes begin to flutter open and they struggle to see Henry in the dim light. "Henry, what time is it? What are you doing here so late?"

"It could not be helped, Da. It is three o'clock in the morning and I came to tell you that Anna has made me a father and you a grandfather. I have a little girl, just as beautiful as her mother, Da. She is very early, and very tiny but she is perfect and Anna is perfect. Da, do you understand what I am saying?" Da has tears in his eyes and nods yes. "I have one question for you, Da. What do you want Clara Beth Harrick to call you? Papa, Grandfather, Pawpaw, or gramps or something else?

"Oh, I have been thinking about this for a few months now. I want her to call me, 'Pawpaw'. She can call you Da, now. What a beautiful way to wake up. When can I go meet my granddaughter?"

Henry realizes that his father is no longer slurring his words. His face is almost normal again and there is a huge twinkle in his eye. "We will ask Dr. Mason, when we see him again. I must go call Judd and Judy and Matthew. Da, you know I am the luckiest-happiest man alive right now? Don't you?"

"As you should be, you deserve to be, my son. Kiss the girls for me the next time you see them, please. Now go make your calls. I love you, son."

"I love you, too, Da. I am sure that the Master clan will be a visiting in a few hours, so rest up, now, okay? Henry leaves his father's room, feeling as light as a feather.

The calls are made and they were all so surprised and happy at the news. Judy was screaming on the phone for everyone as soon as Henry told her. It almost burst Henry's eardrum but he understands her enthusiasm.

Matthew and Susan were harder to get a hold of. The phone rang about fifteen times before Matthew answered it with, "This better be life or death at this hour."

To which Henry replied, "Definitely, LIFE, little bro. You are an uncle to the most perfect little girl that looks just like her perfect little mama."

"Susan, wake up, Anna had the baby!! Let's get dressed and get to Lawrence. Does Ma and Pa know, already?"

"Yup, called them first, of course. I forgot to tell them that Da is in the hospital. He is doing much better but he had a stroke on Saturday. I should call Judd back."

"I will let him know. I need to call them. They might want to stay for a few days so we may take separate cars. Anna is doing okay, then?"

"It was very touch and go for a while is what Dr. Mason said. He also said Anna might not survive another pregnancy. I do not know if she knows this, yet. But she looks like an angel holding my daughter. Matthew, it feels so odd to say those words. My daughter. Her name is Clara Beth"

"That's a lovely name, Henry. I cannot wait to meet my niece! See you in a few hours."

Henry puts down the receiver and looks over at Carolyn. She is on one of the couches, sound asleep. She had already called the Main house and told Joshua the good news. Henry still feels too happy to sleep, if that makes any sense. He goes to the other couch and lies down on it and folds his arms over his chest. He thinks to himself. *I will just close my eyes and picture my Anna as she was when I walked through that door.* He closes his eyes and is sound asleep in less than a minute.

TWENTY-SIX

October 17ᵗʰ, 1866. Wednesday
An excerpt from Elizabeth Lewis's Journal

Of all the stories that we have heard regarding the Massacre, Uncle killed the most Raiders, and I killed one, also. Out of four hundred and fifty men, only forty were killed during the Massacre. Seventeen of our young boys were killed in the first three minutes, in that tent encampment. It doesn't seem fair, but I guess fairness isn't part of a Massacre, is it?

William Quantrill wanted to make the business district pay for all the slights he perceived. So, he divided three groups of Raiders and sent them down Massachusetts Avenue and a group down each street parallel to it. He wanted to catch any owners running out the back as their businesses and they were burning to the ground. This tactic was very efficient. His Rebels looted everything they could carry before they burned the stores to the ground.

George Holt and J.L. Crane lived above their shoe store on Vermont Ave. They surrendered but were shot down for being 'Missouri killers.' Holt survived the shot in the face.

There was a clothing store owned by a German owner Mr. Pollock. It was cleaned out to the bare walls before he was shot and the store burned.

Addison Waugh slept in the back of Dr. Griswold's Drug store and was shot. William Hazeltine owned a grocery store and he lived above it but ran out the back into the ravine while shots were fired at him. He survived by falling down the sloping hill.

B. Eldridge and Ford, the town's largest clothing store had two seventeen-year-old boys sleeping in it. They were told to open the safe but they needed the key from the owner, Ford. They were forced to clothe the constant flow of bushwhackers, when the clothes were all gone, the boys were shot and burned inside the store.

Reverend Hugh Fisher was also on the Death List. He and Senator Jim Lane were Jayhawkers (same as Bushwhackers but for the North) and they did their own raid on the town of Osceola, Missouri in 1861. They led a small band of men to rob, plunder, and set fire just as was happening to us, but no one was killed during the raid in Missouri. Fisher was also known to help runaway slaves. This put him quite at the top of the list. His wife, Elizabeth woke him when she heard the first gun shots. He looked out the windows in time to see his friend and neighbor Reverent Snyder get shot while milking his cow. He took his older boys (ten and twelve) to climb Mt. Oread for cover. He saw that there were men stationed as guards every couple of hundred feet up so he sent his boys up the mountain. He was a very large man with lung problems so he could not make the climb without being seen or heard. He went down to hide in his house. His boys continued to climb, then hid in a cemetery but witnessed several killings.

The Reverend decided to hide in his recently hand dug cellar. Very shortly after he got himself safely tucked away, four bushwhackers barged in the front door, demanding to know where her husband was.

She replied, "Do you think that he'd be fool enough to stay about the house while you are killing everybody you can?" He cursed at her, and called her a liar. She told him not to curse in front of her seven-year-old that was clinging to her waist. She also had a babe in her arms. They searched the house then asked for a lamp to look in the cellar. The leader fumbled with it, but he wet the wick so they needed another lamp. She gave her baby to one of the Raiders and went to the second floor for another lamp. Three raiders tried to see into the cellar with the lamp throwing funny shadows on everything but they never saw the Reverend. When they came back up, they proceeded to set fire to the house. Once again, the wife handed her baby to the raider while she went to fetch water to put out the fire.

The Raider who was holding her baby, said that he would help her save anything in the house but that the house must be burned down because it was on the list. The other Raiders left him to watch her. She tried in vain to put out all the fires and made an excuse to go down to the cellar to call to her husband to escape. He used a dress to hide himself in and rushed out the back door. Mrs. Fisher thought quickly and told him to lay by the far tree as she went in the house to get an expensive rug and she covered him. Then she and another neighbor went in to grab chairs and other small furniture to 'save' and put them all on or near the carpeted reverend. He laughs about it today. He was saved by a Persian Rug! He does thank God, daily, for his wife's determination and presence of mind throughout the whole ordeal.

TWENTY-SEVEN

October 18th, 1866 Thursday
An excerpt from Elizabeth Lewis's Journal.

My family is so important to me. Today is my birthday and my William gave me another journal and a new set of the finest quill pens. Each of my children gave me a handwritten note as a remembrance of the day. Will Jr., about to be seven-years-old has struggled in school with his letters but Lizzie helped him and he was so glad to have written a card, that he read to me, proudly. Young Will is so much like his father, more than even Ian. He is very tall for his age and has a large frame, and light brown eyes. He is very protective of his sisters. Although Lizzie is six years older, he is about even with her height, he has taken to calling her his little sister. So, adorable.

Father Clyde and his new bride, the former Mrs. Marilyn Caldwell, gave me a new shawl. I know that Marilyn sewed it, from fabric that I admired at the Ridenour and Baker Dry Goods store. Father Clyde and Marilyn were married last year, and built a little house for themselves on the other side of the stable. An unusual blessing because of the Raid. Mrs. Caldwell lived in Leavenworth and was on her way to visit her daughter in El Dorado, when the Massacre started. She stayed at the Eldridge Hotel, became my Mid-wife then brought me home. She stayed with us for a month. She made meals, helped with the laundry, tended to Ian's medical needs and mine, and most important, made William's Father smile. After she went back to Leavenworth, Marilyn and Father Clyde wrote each other daily and saw each other every other month. He finally convinced her to leave Leavenworth and come down here as his bride. The ceremony was lovely and her daughter and family all came to town for the occasion. Mary has two young ones but her husband was killed fighting the Confederates in Atlanta.

My young Willie is completely smitten by her Mary's daughter, Julia. She is a year older but very petite. Willie stopped talking and eating and just stared at her, for the whole time that they were here. Mother Marilyn has talked Mary into coming to live here in Lawrence so she can help with her little ones, while she helps me with mine. Wait until Willie finds that out! He will be so excited. He has already asked Lizzie if she could help him write to her, thinking that like Father Clyde, it will lead to love on her part. I love all my children but I cannot help but notice that Willie's heart is as large as his father's and he is never afraid to show affection. More than Ian or Joseph did at his age, anyway.

I haven't said much of my William's part in the day. I mentioned that he was in General Ewing's command and got to Lawrence just in time to find Joseph carrying Ian down Massachusetts Ave. He had been on a horse for eight hours trying to get from Leavenworth to stop Quantrill. His company doctor saved Ian's life by taking off his leg. He was shot in the back of the knee and it was unrepairable so they cut it off just above the damage. It breaks my heart that he was calling for his mom and I wasn't there. I still did not know if he was dead or alive when he going through that ordeal.

Once the Raider's left, Senator Jim Lane had come out of his cornfield hiding place still in his nightshirt and pants (his house burned to the ground, before he could change) and he called for the surviving men to form a Militia and go after the hoard. They were close on their heels since Quantrill ordered his men to burn their way out southeast. When Lane was very close, he became aware that Major Plumb (with my William) was advancing parallel to him. They could soon overtake Quantrill's men if they simultaneously rush in to head off their advancement. Lane, himself went to Plumb to ask if they could work together. Plumb was hesitant because he did not want to take orders or even suggestions from a Militia man. Unbeknownst to them all, one hundred and eighty soldiers were about six miles behind them.

Quantrill ordered George Todd to Captain a rear fighting guard. Eighty more militia men arrived on fresh horses to help Jim Lane and Maj. Plumb. They did attack the rear but it did little to hold them back. They attacked, then retreated, then attacked again and advanced. Todd was very good at defending his Colonel. The three groups of men fought for hours as the main group of Quantrill's Raiders got farther away.

Major Plumb said that he could not have done as much without my William's continued determination to go forward and stop Quantrill. For all his efforts, though, he was shot. It was just a flesh wound, but he bled terribly. He insisted that he be bandaged quickly, so he could get back on his horse. It just grazed his cheek and ear. He has a lovely scar on the right side of his face and his right earlobe is missing. I think the scar makes him look even more dashing. After he healed some, he decided to grow a moustache with handlebars to hide the scar. I like William in a moustache but the handlebar look was too much for him. He is a large man but it made his head look too big for even his large body. Not that he is overweight, he is six feet six inches tall and weighs a mere 175 pounds. The Army weighed him when he signed on and when he was released.

Not that he will not get there, if Father Clyde is an example. Father Clyde is just as tall but more than twice his width. They are cut from the same cloth as is Ian and Willie. I think Willie with be taller than them all.

I remember when I first brought William home to meet my parents. Neither of my parents were very tall, and I am only five foot and three inches. My mother worried that the fifteen-inch height difference would somehow break me on our wedding night, or cause me to die delivering his children. I almost died of embarrassment when she took me aside to tell me of her worries late one night.

My daughter Carolyn is named for my dear departed mother. If the babe in my womb is a boy, I will name him for my Father, Charles. He will be Charles Palmer Lewis. If it is a girl, I'd like to name her Danielle Polly after my Uncle, Daniel Palmer. I have a feeling that it will be a boy, though, I am carrying low and very large. It will be another boy built just like their father.

TWENTY-EIGHT

Wednesday, October 20ᵗʰ, 1937
In EL Dorado, Kansas

In Lawrence, Anna's family have been staying with the Lewis Family. The came separately on the day Clara Beth was born and visited with the mother and babe and the new Pawpaw, Frank.

Dr. Mason allowed Frank to get wheeled in to see Anna and the baby. He was there when the Master's descended upon the little room. A few hours later, Joshua brought the Colonel to see his new great-grand-daughter, as Carolyn calls Clara. Judd and Judy were going to stay for a week but the other Masters had to go home that night, because they all had to work in the morning.

Judy cooks and takes care of the Colonel and bakes and prepares to spoil her daughter and first granddaughter. Today is the day that the baby comes home! Anna and Henry will stay at the Main house so everyone can lend a hand. Anna and Henry are very nervous about being parents for the first time, but they know they have lots of loved ones to help or give advice. Carolyn greets them with the news that they read Great Gram's journal entry for the Eighteenth and it was Beth's birthday! Anna and Henry could not believe that the woman that they named their daughter for was born on the same day as Clara Beth!

Back in EL Dorado, Melinda is at work at The Kroger Grocery. She is filling the details to Joan and Old Petro, of her tiny new niece. Joan remembers how sickly one of her twin granddaughters were being born early and weighing only four pounds also. Today, little Athena is a healthy two-year old and only just slightly smaller than her older twin sister, Diana. Melinda and Joan are lost in their conversations when the register bell rings, which means a customer needs to be rung up. Melinda goes to the register and is shocked that the man standing in front of her is John Walker.

"So, I just heard you say that Anna and Henry have a little one. What is her name, Melinda?"

Melinda just turns and walks toward the meat counter and yells. "Petro, bring your meat clever, we have trouble up front."

"I'm allowed to shop for groceries, Melinda. You have no reason to be mean to me." He follows her deeper into the store.

Petro is out from behind his counter in a split second. "You are no allowed to buy in this store. We have the right to NOT SERVE MURDERERS. Now get out or you see the business end of cleaver." Pete warns in his thick Greek accent.

"No one has been murdered. I have been cleared of that since Anna is alive." John tries to act innocent.

Melinda cannot be silent any longer and addresses John for the first time. "Anna's first baby would have lived if Anna wasn't all busted up during her pregnancy. When you left Anna for dead, you killed that baby! You are a murderer, John Walker."

"I think I will go for two in a row, then?" John says as Petro raises the cleaver. He moves to block the doorway so that John cannot pass to leave.

"Joan, call sheriff, I heard Scum threaten Anna's baby! Stay right there or I cut you. I promise."

The sheriff deputy came but they let Walker walk out unmolested. They say that he did not do anything wrong. Talk is just talk. Melinda gets on the phone to the Main house and when Henry answers the phone she says, "Thank God, you answered the phone Henry, John Walker just came in the grocery store and heard me telling Joan about Clara Beth. Then he threatened to make her your second DEAD baby!"

Anna was on the upstairs hall phone and screams. "Why, why my babies?" She is holding onto the telephone stand. "Melinda why?" Anna pleads.

Henry is in control and asks, "Melinda, have you called the sheriff?"

"Yes, not that it helped. Old Petro had him cornered with a meat cleaver but the sheriff let him go. They said 'talk is just talk'! Henry, he can look up the Legacy Plantation in any phone book. You should take Anna and the baby someplace safe until John is behind bars. The trial is almost over. He has to be convicted!"

"I will call the District Attorney and see if he can go

before the Judge. He has you and a respected business owner as witnesses to the threat, maybe he will withdraw his bail."

Anna cries into the phone. "Henry, I am scared. What are we going to do?"

Melinda speaks. "Anna, Henry has the right idea. Going to the D.A. is the first step. Keep calm, okay? Listen, I must go. I am on the store's phone. I will call you later, or if you guys decide to leave. Call us and let us know? Okay?"

"Thanks, Melinda. We will let you know."

After he hangs up, he picks the receiver back up and dials the District Attorney's office in EL Dorado. Anna comes downstairs with Clara Beth in her arms and goes into the dining room to listen in on the Henry's call. In a few moments, Judd, Judy, Carolyn and Joshua are all in the dining room, listening.

"Thank you, Mr. Pollack, let us know." He turns to the family around him. "Mr. Pollack is going straight to the Judge and see if they can revoke his bond. Melinda and Petro might be needed to testify as to the threat. I do think that we should go somewhere, so we are safe."

"I just got home with Clara Beth. I want to stay home. Why is he doing this?" Henry looks at Anna. She is holding the babe close to her chest. Even with her worry and stress, Henry thinks, she is still the picture of loveliness.

"He is sick, Anna. That is the only reason. He is a sick mad dog! I do not want to leave here but I will have you in a safe place, where ever that is. Any suggestions, anyone?"

They all look at each other. "How about a hotel in Topeka? He'd never find us up there with all those people." Anna suggests and as their eyes meet, Anna smiles, as she always does when her Henry looks in her eyes.

"My great-uncle Chilly has a little cabin near Leavenworth. I have a key to it. I can call him and see if you can use it for a few weeks." Josh offers.

Henry responds, "That's a great idea, Joshua but I think I like the crowded city idea better. We might not need to do anything until we hear from Mr. Pollack."

So, they wait. Judy takes Anna and the baby back

upstairs. It is time for Clara to have a meal. After a few minutes, Judy goes back down and into the kitchen to start dinner. She looks at the clock. *Wouldn't the court be closing about now*, she thinks. She goes to the sitting room to check on the Colonel. He is sleeping in his chair and a fire is roaring.

She puts her hand on his shoulder and he stirs. "Rosanne?" Judy shakes her head. "Oh, Judy, did you know that you look just like Rosanne?"

"So, I have been told. Anna is feeding the baby, I was wondering if you need to use the facilities, Colonel. I have time to assist you before I start supper."

"No my dear, my Julia helps me go by myself. I will go now, though, now that you mentioned it." He gets up with just a little assistance from Judy. What a pair they make. Judy is five foot nothing and the Colonel was six foot six inches just like his father. He has shrunk in height with aging but next to Judy, he looks every bit his full height.

The phone rings and Henry answers it on the first ring, because he has not left its side since he hung up from the D.A. "Lewis Residence, Henry speaking." Henry is silent for a half a minute. "What shall we do? He threatened my newborn." A minute more goes by. "Yes, sir. I cannot believe he can get away with this." Henry sits down on the dining room chair that he has next to the sideboard. "Mr. Pollack, they must find him! I am going to take Anna somewhere safe. I will contact you when we are in hiding. Good-bye"

By the time he is off the phone, he has everyone surrounding him. Joshua, Carolyn, Judd, Judy, and the Colonel all have eyes on him, for the news.

"The Judge agreed with revoking John's bond. They sent sheriffs to his house, but he's gone. They will keep a watch on his house in case he shows up. The neighbors said that before he left, he tore up his house and was screaming at someone but no one saw another person. Mr. Pollack thinks he has gone off the deep end, again! He suggests we arm ourselves and leave – go into hiding."

Anna is in the doorway. "We are not leaving. I will not live on the run. He will trip up. He is not smart and he is not careful. Let him come here to get us. Call the police and set up a trap for him."

There is a car horn beeping outside. They all gasp. Henry looks to the Lewis's. "Do you have any guns here?"

Judd is peeking out the parlor window. "It's Matthew's car. It's Matthew, and Melinda and Susan and Mark!" Judd opens the door.

Matthew bursts through the front door like a ramrod. "John's loose and crazed. We must get Anna and the baby out of here."

Anna says, "We were just discussing that. I think we should set a trap for John. If he is dumb enough to come up here, let's be ready for him. How did you guys get here so fast?'

"Melinda called everyone as soon as she hung up from you. We just got in the car and came." Matthew answered.

Susan speaks, "Matthew drove very fast. He didn't stop when I got sick, either. He just handed me his work hat to vomit into. Disgusting thing to do to a perfectly good hat, might I add. I tossed it out the window. Then I asked Mark if he had a hat on him, in case I felt the urge again." She laughed. "He handed me his good hat, his expensive Fedora, just in case. He was always a great brother-in-law. Handed me his Fedora!" She repeats.

"Then, you don't know, the Judge did revoke John's bond. The sheriff searched his house and he could not be found."

Carolyn comes into the room from the dining room. "I just called Eddie. He said that we could stay at his house. Us girls and the baby, that is. He wants to come down here and help trap John."

Joshua says, "I always liked that guy!" Carolyn elbows him. "Is he on his way, then?" Carolyn nods her head.

"He should be here in a half an hour. Now, Joshua, Henry asked you about guns. I only know of the Colonel's rifle he has on the wall above his fireplace in his bedroom."

The Colonel comes into the parlor from his sitting room. "There is a lockbox in the attic. It has several rifles and five handguns. But do any of you know how to shoot?" Everyone is stunned by the Colonel being so lucid.

Judd speaks up. "I do and I know that Frank taught Henry. I never had a chance to teach Matthew because he was too young when we lost our farm. I did teach Anna how to shoot. She was pretty good, too."

Henry looks to his wife. "I never knew that."

"You had moved away, when Pa showed me how. He thought it would take my mind off missing you. He took me hunting several times." Anna explains.

The baby upstairs is crying and Anna puts her hands to her chest. She is trying to cover the immediate response her breasts have, to the hungry infant upstairs. She looks down and there is milk coming through her bra and blouse. She excuses herself and runs upstairs.

"Joshua, do you know where the lockbox is? I've been to the attic a lot lately and I don't recall seeing it." Carolyn asks.

"That is because I moved it to my room when I came home after graduation. Colonel, you have the key, right?"

The Colonel takes his pocket watch out. "It is time for hot tea and a key." He says and smiles. At the end of his watch fob is a small key. He takes it off the fob and hands it to Joshua. "Here my boy. It is all yours. Break out those guns. We are not going to let anyone hurt Anna's baby Clara Beth."

Judy walks over to the Colonel. "Colonel, you called my daughter Anna for the first time."

"Judy, Anna is like a granddaughter to me. And she named her little girl after my sister and my mother. No one is going to harm a hair on their heads while I draw a breath." He turns to go into the sitting room but turns back after a few steps. "Can you make me some hot tea? I am going to go sit in my chair, if you don't mind." And like that, the moment of clarity is gone.

The women head into the kitchen while the men head upstairs to unlock the lockbox. Anna hears them in Joshua's room and after Clara is satisfied, Anna changes her blouse, and with the baby in her arms, she goes to Joshua's bedroom doorway. All the men have different guns and they are loading them. "This is a scary picture. I never thought we'd have a shootout, in this day, and age."

She goes downstairs and enters the kitchen. Judy is just pouring the tea for the Colonel. Melinda walks over and takes Clara from Anna. "Oh, my, has she has gotten bigger in two days?"

"She drinks almost every two hours. Even at night. I am exhausted. How do women with twins do it?" She looks at her little one. "She is changing already. She is so amazing! I cannot believe she is real. Do you know what I mean?"

Susan says, "I hate to be a party pooper but are we all locked up? Don't you think we should go around and secure all the doors and windows?"

Henry and the men all enter the kitchen. "We are in the process of doing that right now." He says as he locks the back door and checks the various windows. Then the front doorbell rings, and they all jump, including Melinda so Clara is startled and starts to cry.

Henry with rifle in hand, goes to the parlor window to peek out. "It is Eddie." He then goes to the front door. "You got here fast, Eddie. Break any speed records on your way down?"

Eddie notices the rifle in Henry's hand and the one in Matthew's. "So we are an armed camp, now? I brought my own." He reaches in his jacket and pulls out a .38 caliber revolver from a holster under his arm. He smiles, he intended this to be a joke but no one is in a laughing mood.

Carolyn goes to his side. "I am so glad you are here Eddie. I know that you said we should go to your place in Topeka but I for one do not want to leave. Who knows if or when this John Walker will show up? It could be a week or a month or tomorrow morning. I am with Anna on this, I do not want to live 'on the run.'"

"Carolyn, always an immovable force. I love you but this is not the time to assert yourself." He says with all seriousness.

"Say that again."

"I said that this is not the time to assert yourself."

"No, the thing before that"

He smiles, he now understands what she is asking. "Carolyn, always an immovable force. I LOVE YOU! Is that what you wanted me to repeat? I've said it to you before."

"Yes, when we were alone. Now you've said it in front of everybody." She smiles and goes to him and kisses him, with everyone watching. "I love you, too. BUT, I am not leaving my home while the men I love stay to defend it. I am taking a Gram Beth attitude. We all must do what we must, to survive. We are sticking together. Come see Anna's baby." She leads him into the kitchen where Melinda is still holding Clara and rocking her.

Henry gets serious again. 'Well, we were just checking all the windows and the doors. I've checked the kitchen and laundry and the home office."

Matthew says, "I've checked the parlor and the sitting room. We just have the dining room to go."

Joshua calls his farm foreman Joseph and asks him if he has any laborers that he can call right away. He explains that he needs to post guards at the different entrances to the property. Joseph says he will call Jose and a few other men. Both Joseph and Jose saw Anna broken and unconscious before Dr. Mason put her in the ambulance. They will not let that monster get anywhere near her, again.

After supper, the local Sheriff calls. He got a call from the EL Dorado Sheriff regarding the fugitive John Walker. He told Joshua that he will be doing regular patrols around the house. Joshua asks, "Sheriff is there a security guard agency that I could hire as body guards? Trained professionals, I mean."

"If that's the way you want to go, son. I recommend the Brewster Security Agency. They have all former soldiers, policemen and those type. They are also the largest Agency in this side of Kansas. I have the owner's number here, somewhere. Let me get that for you."

Joshua took down the phone number and called Byron Brewster immediately. Mr. Brewster said that he will come over with a few men in two hours. When Joshua got off the phone, he went into the parlor where the family was all gathered.

"I have Joseph and Jose and a few other men, stationed at the entrances of the property. They have orders NOT to stop anyone but to call here immediately if anyone approaches the house. The Lawrence Sheriff will be making extra patrols around our property. I also called a Security Guard Agency and they will be here in two hours with some men. They will be armed and stationed on the grounds surrounding the house. I am sure that they will have suggestions as far as our safety. We need to listen to these professionals. NO immovable objects or 'I don't want to live on the run' comments. I am hiring people who know what they are talking about, and we must do what they say." He looks at his two sisters, Carolyn and Anna. "Understand?"

"Yes," they both say at the same time. No one says 'Jinx, Double Jinx.'

TWENTY-NINE

October 20th, 1866. Saturday
An excerpt from Elizabeth Lewis's Journal.

Mrs. Caldwell, now Mother Marilyn, was a true force to be reckoned with! She got me home, and in my own bed in no time at all, that morning of the Massacre. She saw that I had started breakfast before leaving out and finished cooking it and fed Lizzie and William (they only had sweet cakes at the Eldridge).

Father Clyde was the first to make it back home. He came out of his root cellar hiding place and saw the Union troops and found out it was his son's Company and was led to him. Ian was already in surgery. He then went to the business district to find Uncle Daniel. As he stood in front of the burning Gun Shop, he joined the bucket-brigade trying to put out the flames. The wives from across the street had already spread the word of Uncle's heroism and his demise. When Father Clyde heard, he broke down crying for the loss of his best friend. (As I said big hearts reside in these large men.)

When he returned home to the smell of fresh cooked food, he was in no mood to eat. Mother Marilyn, told him of the loss of the baby and his brother, Charles. This just about undid him. But he had good news of my boys and his son, so he gathered his courage and came to me in my sick-bed. I do not recall any of his words but I know that he held my hand and we both cried for our losses. I started to rise, because I wanted to go to Ian. He and Mother Marilyn would not hear of it. Father Clyde said that he would go back to Ian and stay with him and let Joseph come home. Joseph had insisted on staying at Ian's side and even assisted in the operation. To this day, Ian chides him by calling him 'Saw-bones Lewis'. Two boys could not be any closer friends.

Father Clyde did eat something before going back to town, and Joseph did come home. Father Clyde spent the night with Ian and brought him home the next day.

There was little time to think about our losses. We had family to bury. Of Uncle and Levi, all that could be found were skulls. Mrs. Gates and I were each given one but she suggested that Levi and Uncle be interred together, so that we were sure that we had the right one named. We had lumber on the farm enough for one full sized casket for Father, one third size for Uncle and Levi's remains and one tiny one for my baby Clara. We donated the rest of the lumber to the town for other caskets. Father Clyde built ours and got to work helping others build theirs. There were very few men left alive with carpentry skills, or tools.

It still amazes me that our town survived and flourished through this time. Two-thirds of downtown Lawrence were homeless. There were no stores left to buy clothes or groceries.

Many people had their valuables stolen and / or had their breadwinners killed. We, like many of our farming neighbors, sent food to the town hall to be given out to those in need. Wagons loaded with provisions came in from Topeka, Leavenworth, Wichita, Wyandotte and other big towns as soon as the next day.

St. Louis, Missouri, raised ten thousand dollars for the city to be loaned out for the rebuilding of businesses at no interest. As the businesses began to repay these loans, the monies will be regenerated for others to borrow.

The first to begin rebuilding was the Ridenour & Baker Groceries. Though Ridenour's home burned down and Baker was lingering between life and death, business resumed the first week after the Massacre. W.E. Sutcliff had a very expensive clothing business and his new store was better and his stock was more extensive than ever. J. G. Sands' Harness Establishment had his wood-constructed store burned and he rebuilt in brick and stone. His advertisement for many years was "Established in 1855; Stood in Drought in 1860; totally destroyed in 1863; defies all competition in 1864!" That is the attitude of so many businessmen here in Lawrence.

Once all the affected people had applied for loans to rebuild, the funds will be made available to the children of the victims for their education. My Ian (being seriously wounded) qualifies for a college loan through this fund. He decided that he wants to stay on the farm and take it over one day. (Joseph wants to be a doctor but he will not qualify for a loan through this fund.)

People who still had homes were very generous and took in neighbors. People opened their homes, pantries and closets for those in need. The borrowing of furniture and clothing was enormous. The heat of that summer, quickly turned into the chill of winter but many neighbors were still housing neighbors.

You have no idea; how many good people did a great many things in our time of crisis! I am in awe of the goodness in my fellowman. What an unexpected by-product of those horrendous hours!

THIRTY

Thursday, October 21st, 1937
In Lawrence, Kansas

Judy and Judd are up and in the kitchen to begin breakfast for everyone. There are many mouths to feed and supplies are running low. Anna is the chief inventory clerk but she has been otherwise occupied. As Judy is pulling food out of the icebox, she is calling out things that need to be ordered to Judd who is writing things down.

Anna is the next person in the kitchen. Judy goes to her to take her granddaughter. "Anna, did you get any sleep? You look so tired."

"Ma, I never knew what tired was before I had Clara. She not only drains me of milk but of energy, as well. I need to wash diapers and put them out on the line. Will they let me go outside, do you think?"

She is referring to the Security Guards that came late last night. Joshua is paying for a 24 hour – 4-man team to keep guard on the four corners of the house. "How are we going to live like this? I feel trapped, already. And who is to say that when you all go back to EL Dorado. He won't try something to you or Melinda or Matthew or Susan? You all cannot just stay here in this armed encampment."

Judd puts his loving arms around his first born that is a taller beautiful copy of his lovely wife, "Anna, the sheriffs are all looking for him, in both towns. They have a warrant out for his arrest. I do not know if Mark and Matthew plan on staying but there is safety in numbers. Joshua was talking to the owner, Byron, about being more aggressive looking for Walker, and tracking him down. Your Lewis family, your Masters family and your Harrick family are all here for you, my baby girl."

"Oh, we have to call and see how Frank is doing this morning. He could be in danger, too. He will be better off here if he can be released!" Henry walks into the room, looking just as tired as Anna. "Henry, we have to get Da home! We don't know if John will try to hurt him? Everyone you and I love are in jeopardy. I will go call Dr. Mason. He will bring him home in an ambulance like when he brought the Colonel home for our wedding, especially if I ask him."

"I know that he would but only if Da is stable enough. I do not think he is. Let's go call, they might be able to put a guard on his door, at the very least."

Anna and Henry disappear into the dining room. Judy hands Judd, baby Clara and she starts frying the bacon. "Judy, I haven't put the coffee on yet. Carolyn will need that first thing."

"Yes, you are right, coffee first. We do not want Carolyn out of sorts for the want of coffee! I will get right on that. Judd, you still look handsome with a babe in your arms." She stops what she doing to give him a peck on the cheek and she gives Clara's head a peck, also. "Are we going to get through this, Judd? I am worried."

"Judy, you were the one who knew that you were not going to see Anna again, before she disappeared. What are you feeling?"

"Just worry, nothing else."

"Then everything will be just fine. I am not saying it will be easy, but nothing serious is going to happen to our family. I am as sure of that as I am sure that this little girl is a blessing from above."

Judy wipes a tear from her eye and turns to start the coffee. "She is that, isn't she? A perfect blessing from above."

As if she knew that they were talking about her, a minute earlier, Carolyn comes into the kitchen. "I don't smell coffee, what's the hold-up? How am I supposed to start my day?" She smiles as her attention is refocused on the baby. "Never mind, I just switched my morning fix. May I hold my niece?" Judd carefully hands her over, with a smile. "She is a ray of sunshine, isn't she?" Judd turns to work on the coffee.

"Unless, she is hungry in the middle of the night. My Anna is exhausted. I hand her over to Anna for a feeding and that is enough to make me feel like the walking dead. Anna is not only waking but being the sole source of the nourishment. I wish I could do more to help her." Henry says as he comes back into the room. "She went to go get Clara's diapers for washing. Da is not stable enough to come home but Dr. Mason said that he will have security posted at his door."

Judy asks what does everyone want, for breakfast and gets started on it. Anna comes downstairs with a large full basket full of cloths and goes straight into the laundry room. She loads everything into the wringer washer and starts the machine. When she is done, she comes into the kitchen and says to Henry, "I need to go to the Little house and get a few things. Do I need to take a gun?"

"One of us will go with you Anna, we will be armed, of course." Offers Matthew who is just entering the kitchen with his bride Susan.

"Matthew, I know how to shoot better than you, you know." Anna teases him.

"I will send you with Susan, she shoots better than me, also." All eyes look to Susan.

"Shooting Galleries." She shrugs her shoulders. "They aren't real guns that kick back. I have shot those also. But I am a marksman at the carnivals."

Melinda and Mark walk in together. Mark says, "When I was courting her sister, Susan would be our chaperone and giving her money for the shooting gallery was the only way, I would get some alone time with Sharon. She would go home with the biggest stuffed animal that they had, each time."

"Sounds just like my adorable wife. How old was she then?"

"Ten or so. She was our flower girl a year later." Mark smiles at Susan. "Good memories." Then he gets a little misty. "Right sis?"

Susan walks up to Mark. "Right big brother." She hugs him and gets a little choked up in the process. "I don't know why I cannot keep control of my emotions, lately." Then she remembers and blushes as her hands go to her belly that hasn't even started to pop, yet.

Finally, Joshua, Eddie and the Colonel enter the kitchen. Anna says, "I didn't hear the bell. Good morning Colonel, did you sleep well?"

"I called out to Joshua instead of ringing. I wanted to get out early and teach all of you, young in's, how to shoot proper. It is very important if we are going to have all this fire power out into the open."

Everyone looks at each other and the Colonel. He sounds as if he is 30 years younger and very NOT confused. Carolyn, still holding Clara, goes to him. "Grandfather, do you want to hold your Great-Granddaughter Clara?" He holds out his hands.

"She hardly weighs, anything. She is the spitting image of Anna, already, isn't she?" He looks up at Anna, who has never heard him say her real name. "And she looks like Judy, too, of course."

With breakfast, out of the way, Anna puts all the diapers through the wringer then takes the wet basket of diapers to hang out the line, just off the back porch. Henry is with her for protection. They nod to the security man that is stationed by the back door, before beginning their work. "Henry, this seems so surreal. Hanging diapers while I have an armed guard. How long can the Lewis family afford to keep this up? What if John has just skipped town and we never see him again? What if he waits until Clara is in school and we've let our guard down, thinking we are safe? I want him caught, and I want it yesterday!"

Henry stops her hands from pinning another diaper. "We will get him, Anna. One way or another. John's mind will not allow him to wait or just run away. He is too impulsive and sloppy. But in the meantime, look at what extremes everyone is going to for you. For US, I mean. Even the Colonel, has been sharp as a tack, during this crisis. That is so cute and practical, that he wants to teach us shooting!" Henry lets go of her hands and walks over to the man from security and talks to him for a bit. The man nods while listening. Then he points to someplace near one of the farm buildings. Henry shakes his hand and comes back to Anna. "It is set up, after lunch we are all going to have shooting practice. Bob over there will call his boss and have all the equipment we need brought down here. If it wasn't for the reason why we need to do this, this would be fun."

"I agree, I liked shooting with Pa. I even bagged a few wild turkeys when we went hunting." Anna smiles at the memory. "Feels like five lifetimes, ago."

After they are done with the laundry hanging,

Henry, Anna and Joshua all go to the Little house for Anna and Henry to pack some clothes and baby things and what not. Joshua is standing guard on the porch.

Anna looks at Henry. "Last time we were here, we weren't parents, yet. How much has changed in a week! Oh, speaking of change," she looks down at the wet spots starting to show on her blouse. "It must be Clara's feeding time! This leaking is so embarrassing! I need to buy a good nursing bra or two."

"Anna, you are at your loveliest when you are feeding our daughter and you have one shoulder exposed. I wish I could paint so I could capture the holy image of my angels." She blushes.

"Henry, there is no one like you in the whole world and I am so glad that you are mine." She reaches up and kisses him. "If Dr. Mason didn't tell me to abstain for four weeks and Joshua wasn't on our porch, I might have had my way with you, for saying something like that to me." She winks at him.

"Four weeks! He said we can't . . . for Four Weeks? Anna, I don't think I can hold out that long. I love you so much, and right now you are the most alluring, you have ever been."

"Henry, he said I can't have you for four weeks but there are other ways to pleasure each other. We must be a little creative, for a while. I think we will be just fine. Trust me." She winks at him. "You trust me, don't you?" He blushes as he takes her in his arms. He kisses her slowly and softly. She instinctively leans into him and he can feel her wet blouse through his shirt. He holds her tighter, never wanting to let her go.

"Henry, my breasts are too full and sensitive. Maybe after I feed Clara, we can take a little nap together?" He lets loose of her and steps back.

"See, I have no control when it comes to you, my beautiful wife. Let's not keep Clara's meal waiting." She blushes knowing that he is taking her up on her offer.

As soon as they get back to the Main house, Judy is showing Anna the supply list and Anna gives her the phone number of the grocery stores to place the orders for delivery. Judy makes the calls while Anna takes Clara upstairs to her old bedroom for her feeding. Henry follows her and waits patiently. He could watch his wife do this for hours. As little Clara drifts off to sleep at the second breast, Anna motions for Henry to put her in her basket. By the time he gets her all nestled in and covered, Anna has fallen asleep from exhaustion. Henry crawls onto bed and snuggles next Anna and is asleep as soon as his head hits the pillow.

Clara Beth lets them know that two hours have passed. Her diaper is soiled and she is not happy about it. Henry is the first to stir and he tends to his daughter. "How does something so awful come out of something so beautiful." He says as he waves a hand in the air to dispel the odor. Anna is up and laughs at her husband. He replies. "It is true. You give her pure creamy milk and it comes out like mustard gone bad."

Anna is stretching and yawning. "What time is it?" She says but immediately there is the sound of shooting in the back of the house. Anna's face turns white. "Is it the target practice? I hope."

Henry grabs his gun. "I don't know, but stay here and I will go to Jason's room and look out the back window." The shooting sounds orderly so Anna is not alarmed by it until Henry comes back into the room. "There are no targets set up where we talked about. I am still not sure what is happening. Stay here with Clara. Here is a gun for you. Please do not shoot me when I come back. Remember, I am the good guy." He blows her a kiss.

"You are the very good guy. If it wasn't target practice, someone from the family would be running up here to protect me and Clara."

"That is true. Stay in this room and lock the door after me. Anna . . . I am serious." He leaves without waiting for an answer. Anna leaves the bed and locks the door, then picks up her fresh changed baby and gives her a few kisses and holds her tightly.

Henry went down the stairs as silently as he could. He peeked in the sitting room and the fire is going strong and the Colonel is in his chair, undisturbed by the shots being fired. He peeks into the dining room, which is empty. He heads into the kitchen and no one is there, either. He turns back to look in the front parlor. That is empty, also. He looks out the parlor window and sees several cars he does not recognize.

Now he is worried, whose cars, are they?

He goes back into the kitchen, and looks out the window to see where the shooting is. It has been constant, not frenzied but rhythmic. It must be target practice and everyone must be participating, but he still cannot see anyone.

Another strange vehicle drives up to the back door. He beeps three times and Carolyn and Judy come from just out of site to go to the car. This must be the grocery delivery but Henry has not seen this vehicle before. The delivery trucks usually have the name of the store on the side of them. This one does not. The driver gets out and opens the back gate of the truck and hands Carolyn and Judy each a small box while he carries a much larger one. They turn toward the house. Carolyn is talking to the delivery man as she is walking in the door.

Henry interrupts, "Carolyn, what is the shooting? Are they doing target practice? I cannot see anything from any of the windows."

Carolyn can see the gun in his hand and the serious look on his face. "We are on the other side of the far outbuilding. It was your idea. We are all safe."

"I better go up and let Anna know, I made her lock herself and Clara Beth in the bedroom." I hope lots of coffee was ordered. I could use some. He smiles and turns to relieve Anna's concerns upstairs.

Judy says to him as he leaves the kitchen, "I'll get a fresh pot on the stove, right away, Henry. I will make sandwiches for both of you, since you both missed lunch."

Once upstairs, Henry knocks on the door. "Anna, don't shoot, it is your loving husband. Please unlock the door. Your Ma, is making us sandwiches. We slept through lunch." He waits, but Anna does not respond. He cannot hear anything from the room. "Anna, darling, I am getting worried." He waits for another moment. He knocks on the door again. "ANNA, did you fall back asleep?" He knocks a few more time then, starts pounding. "ANNA, answer!"

A voice says from behind him. "Henry, I was in the bathroom. The bedroom door is unlocked. I heard that it was safe and I had to go pee. Clara Beth is sleeping.

Or she was before you got violent with the bedroom door. She reaches past him and opens the bedroom door. Clara was awake and cooing in her basket.

"Anna, I have to say, I cannot live like this either. My imagination thought the worst when you did not answer me." He grabbed her and held her. "I am so afraid of losing you, I am beginning to be paranoid about everything. I almost drew on the grocery guy, because he wasn't driving a company truck."

"That's what I was saying. We must get John off the street and behind bars. Or we will go nuts looking around every corner, suspecting everything and everyone. We must find John as soon as possible!"

THIRTY-ONE

October 21st, 1866. Sunday
An Excerpt from Elizabeth Lewis' Journal.

The first two nights after the Massacre, for the town, was without sleep. So many bodies to find, so many wounded to help. There were only two doctors left alive but they had no medicine. So many men endured very painful removal of bullets while awake. The dead from the business district were brought to the Methodist Church and laid in rows. Those left with intact houses would stay home for their vigils. The heat of the days and those that followed made it necessary to quickly find them all as quick as possible.

I recall being out on my porch after Father Clyde left, Joseph was in the house eating everything Mrs. Caldwell could put in front of him. I sat and looked toward downtown and it was aglow from all the still burning buildings. My William, I was told was on the trail of Quantrill. He still did not know of his daughter's death or the death of my father and Uncle.

The Massacre took place on a Friday. That Sunday many, many people crammed into the Congregational Church for service. Mostly women, many recently widowed, and our children. Many were still in the clothes they had on during the Massacre, because they had no other clothing to their name. The heat and smell of the still smoldering fires, and the blistering heat of the day made the Service feel like we were in Hell itself but we prayed. Reverend Cordley and Judge Carpenter's brother-in-law Reverend Morse officiated. No sermons were said, Reverend Cordley offered prayers up for the dead and read the Seventy-Ninth Psalm:

O God, the heathen are come into Thine inheritance; they have laid Jerusalem in heaps, the dead bodies of Thy servants have they given to be meat unto the fowls of the heaven, and the flesh of Thy saints unto the beasts of the earth. Their blood has shed like water round about Jerusalem, and there was none to bury them."

After a moment or two, we filed out to continue to look for our loved ones, bury them and survive how we must.

Toward nightfall, a farmer on Mt. Oread saw a fire about three miles southward near the Wakarusa River, where Quantrill was last seen crossing. Something was burning, it was a huge fire. It had to be Quantrill, coming back to finish the job he started. The call went out. "Quantrill was back!!" "They are coming, again!!" "Quantrill's coming, again!!" Bells and shouts ran up and down the town while the panic began to build.

People started heading toward the cornfields, gullies and ravines. They became so unnerved that they ran as a stampede of buffalo. Many of the women, brave in their homes on Friday, became hysterical at the thought of facing the men again.

As people hid outdoors, there was a sudden drop in temperature and the wind kicked up. For the first time in the month, it started to rain, with lightening, and thunder booming. Everyone remained in their hiding places all during the night in the cold and rain, fearing for their lives. Reverend Cordley was quoted in the paper describing the ordeal:

"The horror of that Sunday night was in some respects worse than the Massacre itself. At the raid, there was no panic and no outcry. There had been no warning and there was no escape. But this night alarm gave room for the wildest imaginations and the most exaggerated fears. It unnerved the bravest with its undefined dread. In some respects, panic is worse than peril. People who passed through the raid without flinching, were utterly unstrung and demoralized by this Sunday night panic."

The fires turned out to be haystacks burning in Endora. Quantrill was in Missouri but his control of our town was still very real. We felt trapped and thought that he was still lurking behind every dark corner.

We did not have time to feel that way for long. Too much to be done. No time for weeping or wringing of our hands. Our hands were needed elsewhere and everywhere!

THIRTY-TWO

Sunday, October 24nd, 1937
In Lawrence, Kansas

Two more days go by, looking very similar, to the day before. The Lewis family, the Masters' and the Harrick's all live in the armed encampment.

The only exception is that they ask Pastor Jonas to come to the Main House to give a private Sunday service. He is very surprised at how they are living but was very glad that they did not forget to include their weekly devotion to the Lord. When Carolyn called him to ask him to come to the Plantation, Anna was tugging at her sleeve to ask if the Pastor could baptize Clara Beth, while he was here. So, after the service, the Pastor set up for the Baptism. He asked for a large bowl and he brought a pure white small gown and a large container of Blessed Water from his car.

The Ceremony is set up in the front parlor. Joshua grabs a four-foot tall wood plant stand to hold the large bowl. Carolyn lends her finest crystal pitcher as the font. The Pastor fills it with the Blessed Water.

When asked, who will be the God Parents, Anna asks if the baby can have two sets. Pastor Jonas says, "it was not forbidden but that it was very unusual. But this family as always done things in that fashion." The four God-Parents would be Carolyn, Joshua, Melinda and Matthew. Anna said that she could not decide between her four siblings so why not have them all!

The Ceremony itself only takes a few minutes. The Reverend pours the water on Clara Beth's head, asking her if she renounces Satan and all his works. The God-parents all respond "I do". Then he lays the gown over her and pronounces her clean and baptized as the newest child of God's family.

Judy, Anna and Susan are crying. Henry shakes Pastor Jonas' hand and thanks him for granting such an unusual request. "Not at all, Henry, the Lewis family just very generously added to our new roof fund." He says as he pats the top pocket of his jacket where the written check is awaiting deposit.

The women have prepared a feast and invite the Reverend to stay and partake. With the guards, still at their stations, the families almost forget that they are in an armed encampment for a reason.

After the Reverend departs, Mr. Brewster comes to the Main house with some news. "We think John Walker was spotted in Lawrence getting gas in his Model A. I feel we should increase the patrols. Replace your farm crew at the entrances with armed men also. He has come this far. He will surely keep coming." Brewster was a large man, who looked like he had taken more than a punch or two, in his day. But his commanding nature makes you feel safe in his presence.

Matthew speaks up. I think that we need John to think that we have LESS security so he feels safe coming for revenge. Pull back the outward appearance. Have men in hidden places ready to close in. All the cars always surrounding the Main house must disappear. Anna and the baby must seem approachable."

Brewster nods his head in agreement. "We can do that. What's next?"

Eddie says "The house must look empty, also, to lure him in."

Henry chimes in, "Joshua, how close is the harvest of the squash and pumpkins. We can act like we are all going out to the fields. But how will he know that?"

Anna adds, "Advertise – run a full-page ad looking for workers for the harvest. John will see it or hear of it. He will come to join the harvest as a way, to get close to the Main house."

"Brilliant!" says Henry. "I married the woman with brains to rival her beauty!" He winks at her. "But I do not want you or the baby to be here. We need a decoy."

"No decoy, John will not be fooled. It must be me! We can say that lunch will be provided and served at the Main house. John will know that I am the one cooking. He knows I cook! We need to act as if we do not know he is loose and coming for me!"

"All we need to know is when will the harvest be ready. It is a good plan." Says Eddie.

THIRTY-THREE

October 24ᵗʰ, 1866. Wednesday
An Excerpt from Elizabeth Lewis' Journal

Something happened the other night that has me absolutely stunned. I had to wait to write about it until my nerves calmed down. I am not ready for it. I had no idea that this was coming. The babe in my womb seemed to jump around to echo my excitement. I looked to William and he was just sitting there! How could he take this news so calmly?

We were having dinner at the City Hotel. Miss Lydia had sent us the invitation, herself. Since the passing of her father, Nathan Stone, Lydia took over running the Hotel and helped many people in the town with her charitable works. She is a lovely girl of just nineteen but the Massacre has made everyone age out of necessity.

She invited the whole family but I felt that the younger babies were better left at home to a sitter. Lydia did make a point of sending Father Clyde and Mother Marilyn a personal invitation, also.

Lydia had no one else in the dining room but us. I could not figure out why we were being honored so. As the appetizers were being served, she asked if we could bow our heads in prayer.

As we were all bowed, I heard my Ian's voice join hers in saying, "Dear Lord above, thank you for all that you have given us. Thank you for giving us, each other. Please bless our coming Union with all the love and grace we do not deserve. And bless this food set before us as we join our families, together. Amen."

I looked up to see Ian and Lydia standing and holding each other and looking in each other's eyes. I know that look, he is in love! And with Lydia Stone!

"What is going on? How long? When? How?" I was the only one that seemed upset by this revelation. "You love each other?"

They turned to look at me. Ian speaks, "Mother, she is my everything. I have asked her to marry me. She has said yes. We would like to be wed as soon as possible."

"But you are only seventeen. Can you not wait, until

you are older?"

Ian turned to Lydia, who looked down and with the hand not holding Ian's she ran her hand across her belly. I gasped and turned red. I knew what that meant. My Ian was to be a father and I was to be a Grandmother. But I was with child myself! I knew I was too old to be still delivering.

"Mother, we have talked with Reverend Cordley and he said that he will perform the ceremony on Saturday, IF we have your blessing."

"Mrs. Lewis, I will make your Ian happy. I know that I will. I love him so much. He can help me with the Hotel and I will finally have the big family that I have always wanted."

I looked to my William, again. The one time I would like him to say something, he says nothing. "William, say something!"

My William rises to his feet. "What time on Saturday? Congratulations, Ian! Raise a glass to Ian and Lydia." I limply took my cup and raised it to my lips but I could not drink. I felt as if I had no breath left. William looked at me. "Beth, drink to the good news and the blessings that are coming!" I found myself drinking to them. What else could I do?

We have three days left before my Ian becomes Lydia's Ian for all time. My little man with one leg who never let that stop him from living a full life is starting on his journey.

Mother Marilyn has come to talk with me in my room. She thought that knew of my hesitance. "Beth, it is a sad day, when we think of our first one to be married. You had no time to see it happen. If they had been open about their courtship, you would have expected it. We have no choice regarding our child's love life. Just as our parents could not tell us who and when to love." I am shaking my head. I do not know if she understands at all. "Or is it that she is with child so soon and so young?"

"Oh, Mother Marilyn, I am ashamed. It took me so long to have my first born. My Ian. And my Ian will be a father at just barely eighteen. Lydia is a lovely girl and I considered her father a good friend. I am not being fair but I am just filled with a dread. This does not feel like something to celebrate to me. I cannot explain it. I am happy for the couple but I am so sad for me. I am a terrible mother!"

Marilyn seems to understand what I cannot explain and leaves me to my thoughts. I sat down at my mirror and looked my reflection. I saw a bitter old lady before me. Older than being a grandmother for the first time is making me. I forced a smile and my youth slowly reappeared. Just then little Carolyn comes into my room. "Mama," she says. "Mama, up?" I picked her up. She barely fits on my disappearing lap. She pats my belly and says, "Mama's baby?"

I looked at my youngest. "Yes, Carolyn, there is a baby in Mama's belly.'

She looks at me with teary eyes, "No - Me! Mama's baby! Me!" She points to herself.

"Yes, Carolyn, you are Mama's baby for as long as you want to be." That is where my pain lies. Ian no longer wants to be my baby. He wants a baby of his own. I look at my little girl struggling to find lap space. "Yes, Carolyn, you are Mama's Baby!" I tell her to calm her fear of replacement. I kiss her for making me see why I am in such a mood. "Mama's Baby." I say again. If only I was still saying that to my Ian.

THIRTY-FOUR

Thursday, October 28th, 1937
In Lawrence, Kansas

Brewster's Agency was in charge, of hiring the temporary field hands. All of his men, have seen several pictures of John Walker and they are being watchful. The advertisements asked people to pre-register so that the harvesting of the pumpkins and squashes can be started at first light, this morning. Joshua anticipates two or three days of picking the 20 acres. No picking will take place on Sunday, that is the Colonel's birthday and Carolyn has a small costume party planned for him.

None of the men that signed up look like John, yet. There are about fifty additional men and a few women that showed up this morning, in spite, of the instructions. Joshua, Joseph, Jose and Henry all have their hands full organizing the workers on hand. Henry cannot keep his mind on the farm work. He just keeps looking up and down at the lines for the man who could ruin his life.

Mark and Melinda have gone back to EL Dorado. Mark is not taking any chances with his wife. He insists that he will take her to work and pick her up. He knows that John had originally wanted to hurt her, too, but did not get the opportunity. Thank God, he thinks. He and Old Petro will keep a very watchful eye out for Melinda. Petro said that his cleaver is not going to give a warning if John comes into his store, again.

Matthew and Judd are both out in the fields supervising the workers, with their eyes roaming men's faces, also. Worry is showing on all the faces of those that love Anna and want to protect her.

Susan, Judy, and Anna are very busy in the kitchen, working on the first day's lunchtime meal. Bread has been baking for two days, in preparation, and several casseroles were made in advance. Lots of busy work, but not too busy to hold and spoil the little bundle Clara Beth, anytime her eyes are open.

Joshua had Byron Brewster buy Anna a small derringer that Byron calls 'a little old lady gun'. Joshua said that Anna should keep it in the pocket of the apron he wants her to wear. She has had it on her for three days now and it is very comforting to know that she is not totally defenseless. The Colonel laughed when he saw it and said when his sisters were little they shot bigger guns than that. Then, he insisted that he take her outside to practice shooting and reloading so that she felt it was an extension of her hand. He was being so gentle, loving and LUCID. Anna is going to miss this clarity when it goes, she knows that he cannot keep it up for very much longer.

Kate and Juanita, who are Joseph's and Jose's wives, are setting up the tables with Carolyn, just off the back veranda for the lunch service. The ladies will serve the food at one table and the rest of the tables are for the men and women to sit and eat. It is another bright Autumn day, and the temperature is sixty-five degrees. Perfect harvesting weather, Carolyn thinks. Kate and Juanita talk nonstop about their growing broods. Carolyn is quiet, but also keeping an eye out for the evil man who brutally attacked her precious 'sister' Anna. Of course, she would not have a 'sister' at all if not for him, either. She smiles, wondering if she should thank him for bringing Anna to the Lewis property. Life before Anna was so different. She means so much to her whole family, that she could not imagine not having her in her daily life. That is why, I cannot thank him, she thinks. He wants to take Anna away from Henry and therefore, us.

The Colonel had been up since early in the morning and as it is getting close to the noon hour, he is getting very tired and goes into the sitting room for a snooze. He has his fire going and his blanket around him, as usual.

When all the food is ready to be served, Anna goes to her big Bell and gives the signal for "time to eat". Joshua and Henry are going to bring the workers over a truck-load at a time. When Henry unloads his group of pickers, he looks for Anna at the serving table. She is smiling and has her oversized pink sunhat on and she looks as if she doesn't have a care in the world. Perfect cover, for John's trap, he thinks. He must get back in his truck for another round of hungry hired hands but he makes his way to the table to grabs a sandwich and a kiss from his wife. He leans in to give her a peck on the cheek and she raises her cheek for him to do so. He turns to walk away, when she calls him back. "Henry, that peck on the cheek is not good enough." She looks to the line-up of mostly men. "Sorry everyone, but I must take a moment to give my husband a little sugar for his lunch dessert." She grabs his shirt with both hands and plants a big kiss on his lips. It started out as a fast one but their lips did not part from each other. Her arms let go of his shirt and encircle his neck, instead, while her lips warm his, tenderly. She finally breaks away and blushes. "Off to work with you, now, I have my work to do!" She turns back to pick up the serving spoon. "Sorry, folks, a woman's work is never done!" She looks back at Henry, who is just dumbfounded at the girl who once was too embarrassed to hold hands in public.

"Can we do this again, at the next truck-load?" He asks.

"I wouldn't want to spoil you, Henry. Maybe the one after that, we'll see!" She winks at him and he leaves.

There is a man in line waiting for his food, who looks upset at the disruption of the service. "Can we just get our food, already?"

Joshua has just unloaded a group and hears the man. "Be polite, Buddy, or you will be out on the road without pay. We are feeding you as a bonus, so watch your manners!"

The man, though several inches taller than Joshua, looked as if he was going to object, he grimaced at Anna but then said, "Sorry, ma-am, please blame my stomach for my ingratitude. I haven't eaten in a day or two." He looks down.

"Well, sir, let me give you an extra sandwich, then. I remember what is like working in the fields on an empty stomach, it wasn't pleasant, that is for sure."

After an hour of serving, most of the men had been fed and Anna felt it was time to go feed Clara. She does not want to be in front of all those men if her milk starts coming in and leaking, again. She leans to her Ma and tells her that she is going to the house to feed the babe. Right on cue, she starts to leak, so she hurries into the kitchen where Kate is watching the sleeping baby. "She is still sleeping? I'm surprised, she usually tells me when it is time for her to eat." She leans over and picks up her little girl. "Clara Beth, my little beauty, Mama's going to feed you."

Clara opens her eyes sleepily. Anna does not want to go all the way up the stairs so she goes into the servant's day room, just off the kitchen. There is a bed and a chair in there, and Anna can look out the back window at all the workers eating, while nursing.

By the time Clara is full and back asleep, the women are bringing what little food there was left back into the kitchen to be saved for tomorrow. They have everything cleaned up and are back to baking and the food prep for the next day of feeding the hard-working pickers.

Joshua had said on his last run back out to the fields that almost half of the harvest is done, so tomorrow, Friday, will be the last day of the season. Anna thinks that, it will be the last chance of catching John, also.

It is after dusk when all the men come into the house. They are exhausted from hard work and worry. Henry goes straight to Anna, "I thought John would have showed himself today. If he doesn't try something tomorrow, I do not know what else we can do to flush him out."

The Colonel comes into the kitchen and looks at Anna, "Rosanne, can you put some hot water on for tea, please? Henry, John was here today and with friends. Do we have any cookies left?"

Anna goes to the Colonel, "I will put the water on as soon as you tell me how you know John was here."

Then she answers her own question as he also says, "Julia!" He smiles, "Yes, she told me he was here with 2 other men. They were at lunch, too. But John stayed in the fields. He did not come near the house."

They all look at the frail old man before them. No one can hardly believe him. Anna speaks, again. "Are you sure, Colonel, that it was John that she saw?"

"She told me that if he came into the house that she will tell me so I can protect you, Anna. Julia thinks you are special and she loves Clara Beth, too."

Anna reaches up on her tippy toes and gives the Colonel a kiss on the cheek. "You tell Mrs. Julia, that I have always thought she was luckiest woman to have had you as her husband. And thank her for me, too."

"Yes, I will. Can you see if there are any cookies left? I would like to have them with hot tea, please. Thank you, Rosanne." Without waiting for a response, he shuffles off to the Sitting Room.

It is nearly eight o'clock before the weary families have their supper in the dining room. It has been a long day for everyone. Joshua goes outside to confer with the security detail and lets them know that John might be here with two friends. He cannot tell them where he got this information. They would never understand the Colonel's 'Julia' conversations. Anna is the first person to believe he sees her and talks with her, but if Anna believes, then he does too!

There is little talking at the dinner table or afterward. Everyone is too exhausted. They all go to sleep as soon as the meal is cleaned up.

THIRTY-FIVE

October 28th, 1866. Sunday
An Excerpt from Elizabeth's Journal

Sunlight streamed through the eastern windows, this morning brighter than we've seen it in days. I could not rise and shine but it was not for the want of it. My time is soon approaching. I was getting a deep pain or two throughout the night but I am not due for more than a month from now. I need to stay in bed to keep the baby in place until he is stronger and can live once born. He is big enough but may not be fully developed this early. I cannot go through losing another baby. I am petrified of going through that again. I only survived the loss of my Clara because the children needed me.

William had Lizzie go for Mother Marilyn. Both my daughter and Marilyn came rushing into my bedroom, worried about me. "I think that yesterday's activities were too much for me. I will lay in bed all day, maybe just write about the wedding." I said to them.

It was such a beautiful day for my Ian and his new bride! I wanted to write about it last night but it was nearly 2 o'clock in the morning before we all arrived home.

Yesterday morning, Ian was a bundle of nerves. He was not the only one, either. I, myself could hardly believe that my little boy was going to take a wife. We woke up to thunderstorms and we all thought that it was an ominous sign. I was making the morning meal while William was waking the children. They did not want to rise for there was a damp chill in the air and the thunder and lightning made them want to hide under the covers. Marjorie and Carolyn, who share a little bed held each other so tight that when William picked them up to bring them downstairs, they were still stuck together.

Joseph was very nervous, he was to be Best Man, at only fifteen-years-old. He has mixed emotions, like myself. His best friend in the world has found a new life that doesn't include him. Or so it feels. Young Willie was nervous, also, but for a different reason. Mother

Marilyn's grand-daughter Julia will be here from El Dorado for the wedding and he is smitten by her. To see my funny, talkative, oversized, seven-year-old become a mute is almost laughable.

Lizzie has taken it upon herself to be the one to advise Ian on all the things she thinks a good groom or husband should do or be. She is going to make a commanding little wife and mother someday. I do not know how I would manage without her. As she always does, she has taken charge of the girls' getting ready. She lovingly wrestles them into their pretty store bought dresses and fixes their hair. (Willie even went to her to fix his. This is the boy who has never taken a liking to baths or nice clothes or keeping himself presentable in any way!)

Father Clyde and Mother Marilyn came in before breakfast. Marilyn helps me cook and feed my ever growing, ever hungry family. She had on a new store bought dress also. There was no time for us to sew anything new. Of course, with a large baby in my belly, I could only find dresses that resemble an odd shaped tent!

We were all fed, dressed and the rain stopped by nine a.m. There is an old wives' tale about the sun coming out to meet the bride after a heavy rain being the best luck. William pulled the carriages around and we were off to the Wedding! Ian sat next to me and held my hand. I was very close to crying. He sensed it and put his arm around me. "Mother, you will always be my first love. Lydia is my soul-mate, not a replacement for you in my heart, any more than that babe in your womb is the replacement for me in yours. I will still work on the farm while Lydia runs the Hotel. I am not going anywhere." Then he kissed my forehead. I did such a good job raising this boy! Or he turned out great, despite me, I do not care which, I love him so!

Lydia had her staff decorate the Church with streamers and flowers everywhere. She would have had to send for them from somewhere south, for they were varieties that have bloomed and withered in the fall temperature in these parts. Reverend Cordley was waiting for us. He took Ian off to a small room so he wouldn't see the bride before the ceremony. Lydia was in the larger room in the back of the church and she called me to her side. "Mother Beth, I would be honored if you could help me with my head-piece and veil." As I was assisting her, Lydia looked at me with tears in her eyes, "I wish my parents could be here to see me get married." My heart went out to her, she had said that she wanted/needed to have a large family around her. She picked the right one, too. She will never want for a mother if I have a breath, left in my body.

Lizzie came in and said that a photographer was here for the newspaper. This made the calm Bride start to shake. "I don't like to have my picture taken. They took so many pictures of me after the Massacre, because my father was friends with Quantrill. That was such an awful time."

"Lydia, I was Quantrill's friend, too. But we could not have known what he was going to become. We've both suffered just as much at his army's hands as if we never knew him. I did not think it was right that you were singled out, so." I gave her a hug, though it was awkward with my bulging belly.

The Bride walked down the aisle on my William's arm as a stand-in for her father, my friend, Nathan. I could not keep from crying. I looked over to Mother Marilyn and she was in tears, too. Looking around the room, most of the married women were in tears. We are a sentimental lot.

The Reverend read from Corinthians. Then he explained that it was talking about God's perfect Love for us but that it was the depth of love that each husband and wife should have for each other. He put it so eloquently. My William grabbed my hand and gave it a squeeze. I looked up at him and he was giving me that special look that tells me that his love is that deep. I feel the same for him, always. I gave a silent prayer that Ian and all my children should be so lucky as to feel this kind of love for their spouse after so many years, together.

Before I knew what was happening, the 'I do's' were done and Ian was raising Lydia's veil to kiss his bride. We hastened to the Hotel, where a reception was set-up in the Grand Ballroom. It seemed the whole town showed up to give the couple their regards. Lydia had a large buffet table and the food kept coming for hours.

At sundown, the band started playing and Ian took his bride out to the dance floor. My boy with one good leg and one wooden one, led Lydia in a Waltz. They must have been practicing because they moved perfectly together. After a minute of their solo dance, others started to join in. William took me out to the floor but I could not keep up in my condition. The rest of the dances, William danced with Lizzie on his feet or holding Marjorie or Carolyn. You can be sure that those little ones fell asleep in their chairs with the music still playing from the long day, without a nap.

Joseph and Willie both stood in the back of the room and watched. At one point, Father Clyde had asked his step-grand-daughter Julia to dance. They went around in a few circles then when he was close to Willie, he stopped dancing and asked Julia if Willie could finish for him because he was too old. Julia blushed and said yes and Father Clyde took Willie by the hand and paired him off with her and pushed them out on the dance floor. Willie was very brave and stiffly walked in circles with her. He was trying to imitate the other men but I am afraid that the boy has no sense of rhythm in him. Not that it mattered. Julia was all smiles for her step-cousin. I think she is as sweet on Willie as he is on her! He still does not know that she is moving here. Her mother plans on being here sometime before Thanksgiving.

I do not know where the time went, but it got very late very quickly. A little after midnight, the band announced that Ian and Lydia were going to retire. Several of Ian's friends whooped and hollered and held Ian back after Lydia went into her private quarters. He begged to be free to leave. Instead of letting him go, they hoisted him up in their arms and trotted him about the ballroom several times before ceremoniously depositing him at his bride's door.

You would think that the party would stop when the bride and groom left, but it did not. The band played for another hour and everyone stayed until the very end. I could not believe that Lydia arranged this whole beautiful event in so short a time! I could not have done so with a year to plan.

The ride home was very quiet. The night was a little cool and crisp but my younger children fell asleep on each other as soon as we were on the road. Joseph stayed awake and he, William and Father Clyde all carried a sleeping child to their bed.

I held my youngest, Carolyn, sleeping, against my shoulder to her bed. 'Mama's baby' as she wants to stay. Oh, my little girl, you won't be that for very long. I can feel the heaviness that comes when my time is near. It might be from all the excitement of the day, but I don't think I will have very much longer to wait.

As I was lowering myself into our bed, William turned to me. "It was the perfect day, wasn't it, Beth?"

I let him envelop me in his arms before I sighed and answered. "They don't get much better."

THIRTY-SIX

Friday, October 29th, 1937
Lawrence, Kansas

Everyone is up before dawn, again. There is a flurry of activity. Breakfast is quickly eaten and the men all head back out to the pumpkin and squash fields for the second and final round of harvesting.

More 'new' pickers show up this morning and the Brewster Agency men are looking over the workers with intense scrutiny. Being told that they missed the suspect the day before, heightened their attentiveness to the situation. Things are running as they did yesterday, including the fact that no one has seen John.

Anna, Susan, Carolyn and Judy were up at five in the morning to make pumpkin pies for today's lunch. Susan and Carolyn were cutting up the pumpkins and scraping out the pulp and separating out the seeds. Anna and Judy were making the dough for the pie crusts. Rolling, carving cutting, separating and scraping, lots of hard work being done in the large kitchen in the Main house. Carolyn says, "Why didn't we just order a dozen pies from the grocer? This is too much work."

Anna and Judy look at each other. Anna answers, "Store bought pies? Who does that? Pumpkin bread would have been easier and faster. Carolyn, keep working those pumpkins and we will switch to breads. What do you think, Ma?"

"I think that Carolyn, wants to stop working with the pumpkins, altogether. Right Carolyn?" She turns to look at her. Carolyn is hands deep in a pumpkin and she is working up a sweat. Susan is not looking any happier with her pumpkin seed pile. Judy looks at the two of them and shakes her head.

Susan offers, "I would volunteer to go to every grocer on Massachusetts Avenue and buy every pie or bread they have baked, instead of keeping this up! How about you, Carolyn?" She winks at the taller girl in front of her.

"I'll do you one better, give me the phone and I will

call each grocer and have the baked goods ordered, bagged and if they do not deliver, you can pick them up, one, two, three! Come on, Anna. If we had a week, we could not make enough pies for as many hands as we have picking today."

As Anna opens her mouth to answer Carolyn, Clara starts her cry in her basket in the servant's room. Anna looks down and sees the response her breast give and crosses her arms across her chest to cover the growing milk spots. "Saved by the Clara Beth! Fine, make your calls. This is your plantation, I am just the hired help here, remember?" She is wiping off the flour from her hands and calls out to her little girl, "Mama's coming baby girl. Don't you fret, mama's coming." She hurries to the other room, and Clara Beth stops crying the minute her mother picks her up.

Judy in the kitchen smiles. "These days of motherhood go the swiftest." She says more to herself then to the others. She starts back rolling out the crust for the pies. "This will be the last crust, then. I will take over the carving, while you make the calls, Carolyn. When she makes up the list for you, Susan, you can skedaddle out for those stores. Happy?"

"Yes!" They both answer together. Carolyn cleans off her hands in the sink. "I am off to make some calls!" She literally hops and skips out of the kitchen to go to the phone in the dining room. It only takes a few seconds before she can be heard on the phone with the first store.

Susan says, "I will be glad to get out, anyway. I am beginning to feel cooped up here. Farm life is not for me. I miss my books and the time to read them."

"That's why winter was made, Susan. Long days of snow and being bundled up with a good book and a cup of hot tea."

"Did someone say tea?" It was the Colonel. He got up early with the rest of the household but has been sitting in his chair napping. "Where's the tea?" He looks past all the work and looks at the kettle on the stove, it's not whistling nor does it have a flame under it to get that way.

Anna comes out of the day room with Clara on her shoulder and she is patting her back trying to get a little burp. "I'll get the kettle on, Colonel." Clara makes a loud belch and a toot to match. Everyone in the kitchen laughs. Anna holds her away from her to look her in the eye. "Clara, let this be your first lesson from your mama, Ladies do not toot!" As if she understands, Clara giggles. Anna looks at the Colonel, "Do you want to take her for a second while I get the kettle on?" She hands her precious daughter to the Colonel.

He is very careful with his 'great-grand-daughter'. "You can toot, anytime you like Clara Beth. Better out than in! Just blame it on the dog, that is what I do!" They all laugh. His poor little dog, Robbie, has always been very gassy!

Carolyn comes back into the kitchen. "I have 10 pies being delivered and a dozen needing to be picked up. I think that you ought to take a security guard with you, Susan. John was seen in town, just last week."

The Colonel is still standing with Clara in his arms. He is making funny faces at her and she is still giggling. He looks up at Carolyn, "John is here at the Plantation, not in town."

"Are you sure, Colonel? Did Mrs. Julia tell you that?" Anna asks. The kettle is starting to whistle so she takes it off and pours some over a tea bag, before she turns to him. "Did Mrs. Julia say anything else?"

"My Julia did not tell me but if he was here yesterday, why would he not come back today? Yesterday, he looked about our home and property and has most likely gotten an idea as to when and how to get to you, Anna. At least that is how I would have done it. Don't you think, Clara?" He tickles her tummy and she gives him another giggle and this one comes with another toot. "That dog is at it again!" He replies and everyone just laughs.

"Where did you want your tea, Colonel? We are a little busy here but you can have it in the dining room or your sitting room by the fire, if you like." Anna asks as she pulls out a few butter cookies that he likes with his tea.

He looks at the babe in his arms. "I think that baby has done a little more than toot." He wrinkles his nose. "Robbie never did a smell like that!" He gives her another tickle. "I will go into the sitting room. The air in this room can make a man lose his appetite. Carolyn, can you bring me the tea, please? Anna has a big job to do." He gives her a wink. Carolyn is grateful for leaving the working kitchen, again. She takes his cup and cookies as he hands Clara to Anna and he paddles off without another word.

The last of the pies started are baked and Clara is clean and napping by the noon hour. Susan is back from town with George the guard carrying all the pies. Lunch is nearly ready to be served by all the busy women of the house. Anna gives the Bell signal and waits for Henry to bring the first truck load of pickers.

She has news to tell him, and she is bursting with excitement. She meets him at the door of the truck. "Da called from the hospital and Dr. Mason has cleared him to come home, tomorrow! He will be here for the Colonel's party! I am so glad he will be home. I miss him so much with us being so busy the last few days and not being able to visiting him." She rushes the words out. She needs to get to the serving line to help with the food but she is just so happy to share the news.

"That is the best news, we've had in days, isn't it?" He bends down and picks Anna up by the waist and gives her a swing. "My, you are getting back your lovely figure so quickly. Is that four weeks, up yet?" He winks at her. "It feels like it's been two years since we've . . ."

"Henry, Clara is only eleven days old! And people can hear you, my husband." She puts a finger to her lips to tell him to be quiet. "After the harvest is over, we will have more time to find alternative ways to help each other through this um . . . dry spell." She tippy-toes a kiss. "Now, I really have to get to the lunch table and help feed the workers. Come get a sandwich and macaroni-n-cheese and pumpkin pie before you go get the next load of workers."

As they get closer to the serving line, Joshua's truck is just stopping behind Henry's and when he turns off the motor, the engine backfires. It sounds just like a gunshot. The Security team springs into action and has their guns drawn. Henry has thrown himself between his wife and the sound and has his hand on his gun in his belt. As they all realize the source of the sound, they all ease up. Most of the workers did not even notice the tension that the sound caused. Henry turns to his wife. "See and I almost forgot. We are still in danger. I need to keep my attention on looking for John, not boinking my wife!" He bends and gives her a little kiss on the cheek. "Go to the serving table, I will get a sandwich, shortly." He turns and heads towards Joshua, who is talking with Byron Brewster.

They continue to serve the food for more than an hour. Anna has been watching the faces of the men in front of her with a fixed smile on her face. That backfire scared her, too. Having her family all together and making food for everyone has been like heaven but she too, has taken for it granted. They are in danger.

Just as the last load of workers gets through the line, Juanita comes to Anna to tell her that Clara is awake and hungry. Just the thought of feeding her little one, brings down her milk and she crosses her arms over her breasts and heads to the house, while Juanita takes her spot at the table.

When she enters the kitchen, she can hear Clara crying from her basket on the bed in the servant's day room. She hesitates, looking at the mess that is in the kitchen from all the cooking. "Geez, it looks like a week's worth of cleaning is needed here." She says out loud. Even with her crying, Clara hears her mother's voice and cries out louder to her. "I am coming my darling, mama's coming." She says as she goes into the room to nurse her daughter.

Clara was finished at the second breast and back asleep within minutes. Anna held her to just look at her. "Oh, Clara Beth, you have my heart, baby girl."

"I thought your heart belonged to Henry. Are you fickle, Anna?" Without looking up, Anna loses her smile. This is the voice that haunts her nightmares – *John Walker's voice!* She can feel her heart pounding in her ears. She is not facing him, so he cannot see the look on her face. She knows that her fear must be showing. "Anna, did you hear me?" She puts a forced smile on her face. Then the thought crossed her mind, *our plan worked, he is here.*

She says without turning, "Shush, the baby is asleep." She puts Clara in her basket and puts the basket on the bed. She says to the little one, "There, safe and sound." She finally turns to face him. When she does, she has her little derringer in her hand. She was going to ask him how he got past the security but she saw the tiny moustache that changed his appearance dramatically. "I have been looking forward to this John. I wanted you to see how happy, our life is. You caused us pain, John, lots of it, but we've gotten over it and moved on. I suggest you do the same."

Before John can respond, a voice behind him says. "Anna, is this 'little guy' the one that hurt you?" John spins around and the Colonel is holding a shotgun to him. The Colonel is standing straight and tall and looking like the robust Cavalry man he once was.

"John, looks like we have you trapped, doesn't it? The Colonel and I, have you caught in the middle. Colonel, how did you know, this is John?"

"Julia woke me up. She told me to grab my gun and help you. She shook me hard to wake me, she hurt my shoulder." He juggles the shotgun to one hand so that he could rub the shoulder with the other. John saw his chance. He took a step toward the Colonel. Anna raised her gun but the Colonel got both his hands in the correct position first.

"Hold it right there! I am a good shot and my gun is right even with your head. Now, you tried to kill Anna once and failed. You came here to try again, I assume. I cannot let you do that. Anna belongs here and you do not." He cocks his weapon. "I do not know if you know who I am. So, let me introduce myself. I am Colonel William Clyde Lewis, retired U.S. Cavalry. I was trained to kill little troublemakers like yourself. Now, that was a long time ago and I have not been well, since my Julia passed. But my Julia told me that I could kill you and no one would arrest me because of my illness. Well, I am not going to do that. We, Lewis's live by a code, you see, obey the law, do right by others."

John looks nervously, between Anna and the Colonel. As he starts to say, "I am glad to hear that, sir . . ." He lunges to the bed, where the baby was sleeping. Anna screams. The Colonel shoots, making the baby start crying at the top of her lungs.

"You did not let me finish. The Lewis Legacy is

Family is First." He shouts over Clara's screams. He puts down the rifle and takes the small gun from Anna's shaking hand. "Anna is family to us, thanks to you. Let me see if this little thing can actually, kill a man." He bends over John who is bleeding from his stomach wound, and puts the little gun to his head. "Oh, Julia says that I need to do this, now or she won't visit with me anymore."

"Colonel, let me take Clara off the bed first. I do not want her splattered." Anna says, sounding calm as picks up her writhing infant. John clutches his middle. Anna says to her baby, "There, there, you are safe and sound. Mama's got you and the Colonel is here to protect you." She is rocking Clara, as John just watches from the bed.

Suddenly, in the doorway, are two security men with Joshua. Joshua pleads to his grandfather, "Colonel, I think we can let the professionals take over from here. Anna is safe, you saved her."

John, seeing that he might not be shot, again, grabs for Anna and catches her apron strings and tries to pull her on the bed with him. As Anna is struggling to free herself, two very small shots are fired. She feels the release of her apron and she forces herself to look back at the bed. She sees but turns away as soon as she can. There is not much left of John's face.

She is still rocking the baby. Clara had started to calm down but the extra shots startled her again. Even with Clara's high pitch cry, Anna could hear Henry calling for her. Yelling louder than she has ever heard him call. The little room is crowded now with security men, the Colonel, and Joshua and it is making it difficult to get to the doorway. She calls out, "I am here, Henry. I am okay. Henry, I am fine!"

He rushes into the room. "Anna? Are you okay, is the Colonel, okay? Where is John?" He envelops his wife and child in his arms, kisses both their heads then he starts to rock with Anna to calm down the still crying Clara. He can see past them to the body on the bed and Joshua supporting the Colonel. "Is everyone okay?" Anna just nods her head that is laying against his shoulder. Clara is quieting down. Henry leads Anna out of the servant's day room and into the kitchen.

Carolyn, Judy and Susan are holding each other for support until they see Anna. They run to her and hug her, Henry and the baby.

Joshua leads the Colonel out. Anna hands the baby to Henry and runs to the Colonel and puts her arms around him and with her head against him says, "Colonel, I . . . I . . . owe you my life, <u>again</u>." She starts to cry. "I was so frightened but you were magnificent! John will never hurt anyone again, thank you. And thank Mrs. Julia for me. She saved my life, also. There isn't a Lewis in this house that hasn't saved my life in one way or another." She reaches up to give him a kiss and sees tears streaming down his face.

"I was frightened, too. Julia said that I had to . . . I did not want to take a life but he tried to get Clara by grabbing you. I could not let him touch you. He did too much of that the first time."

Carolyn goes to her grandfather and Anna moves back to Henry. "Grandfather, you should get a medal for this. I can see the headlines, '78-year-old Grandfather saves two lives by killing their attacker!'

Judy speaks up, "your Father and Matthew will want to know you are safe, Anna. I will go call them with your big bell signal. Thank God, everyone's alright!"

THIRTY-SEVEN

October 29ᵗʰ, 1866. Monday
An Excerpt from Elizabeth Lewis's Journal

I was very good yesterday and today. I only left my bed to relieve myself in the chamber pot. My pains are still here and there. Nothing regular, just one or two an hour. They are deep though and I am worried that my body is opening for the release of the babe, but Marilyn examined me and said that I still looked small to her.

Today, Marilyn and Lizzie got everyone fed. Then Lizzie, Joseph and Willie went off to school. Marilyn's grandchildren are still in town so she took my little ones to her place to give me peace and quiet, until school was out. Willie would go straight to Marilyn's after school.

Lizzie came home to check on me. She assisted with the births of her sisters and at thirteen she is very mature. She is interested in being a midwife or a nurse. She and Joseph talk about opening a practice when he becomes a doctor. They are both very serious about schoolwork and get along very well together. I can see them in a small practice together. So, she gave me her nod of approval after examining me. She asked if I needed anything then asked if she could go by Marilyn's to play with the girls.

As the sun was setting, Ian and his bride came to visit with lots of food from the hotel kitchen. When Ian heard that I have been laid up since his wedding, he felt guilty about it. Lydia hesitated at my doorway, not wanted to intrude or disturb. I said, "Come in daughter, I won't bite." Then a deep pain hit me and she could see it on my face. When I looked up at her she was white and looked about to be ill. Of course, she is with child, herself! "Ian, get Lydia a few soda crackers and a cup of cool water. Lydia, come to my side and sit down." They did, as told. When Ian was out of the room, I looked at her and asked, "Lydia, have you been involved in a birthing?" She shook her head no. That is what I thought. This is going to terrorize her just from the foreignness of it. My thirteen-year-old Lizzie has so much more experience than Ian's nineteen-year-old bride!

"Lydia, your mother passed when you were very young. Do you even know the process?" She shook her head, again. Just then, Ian came into the room with the crackers and water. Lydia tried to brighten up for her groom's sake. He looked from her to me with worry on his face. "Ian, we are fine. Why don't you go by Grandfather's and leave us to have a nice long visit? Bring some of that food to them. Poor Gram Marilyn must have her hands full with her grandchildren and all of my young ones, too."

When Ian was out of the door, Lydia started to cry. "Mother Beth, I feel so . . . ignorant. I had no idea that I was even with child or how it came to be. Ian took me to the Doctor because I was sick to my stomach for several mornings. When the Doctor told me that I was . . . expecting, I asked 'Expecting what?' I do not know anything. Ian said that since we had been together, that's what caused it but I am still confused. I am not even sure how the baby comes out!" She broke down to cry and puts her head in her hands in shame.

I struggled to sit up. "Lydia, I will go through it all, and it will embarrass both of us. Let me be a Mama to you and explain it? I have had lots of experience on how it happens, as it turns out." I pointed to my belly and she let out a small laugh. I dove right in, "First off, for a baby to be created, you need a man's seed and a woman's egg . . ." I explained the biology of getting with child and the romance of it. "Do you understand? Do you want to know what happens next?"

"Yes please." She did not look up at me, not once during my whole explanation.

"The baby should take about nine months to grow to the point it wants out. In this case, I am only seven and a half months, so I am trying to keep him in. I may not have a say in the matter. The baby is in charge, of the 'when' part. The 'how' part is different with each birth. The baby is living in a bag of waters and sometimes, it's home bursts and that tells him to come on down. Sometimes the bag doesn't burst until you've been in labor for quite a while. I have had both kinds.

"But I still don't know how or where they come out." She puts her head in her hands, in shame, again.

"They come out the same way the seed went in, Lydia. It all happens between the legs. The normal way to come out is head first. Sometimes they come out feet first, that is called breech. Little Carolyn came out butt first and had her feet up by her mouth, but that's rare. Once the baby is delivered, and the cord from his belly is cut, the bag that held him needs to be delivered, also. It sounds like a great ordeal and it is hard but once you hold your baby in your arms for the first time, you'll know it is all worth it. If it won't scare you too much, you can assist me when this one is ready." I rubbed my huge belly.

"Mother Beth, I am afraid that it will make me more afraid."

"Lydia, it would comfort me if you would hold my hand through it. That is what a daughter does." I reached over and took her hand, gave it a pat then placed it on my belly for her to feel the activity inside. I am not going to deliver just yet. They usually quiet down before the passage out."

Before Lydia could say anymore a whirlwind of chaos burst into the front door. Lydia rushed out of the bedroom to see what the ruckus was about.

William had Willie by the collar and led him straight into my room. Behind him was Ian, Joseph and Lizzie, the boys were each carrying a little sister. "I have never been so embarrassed Beth. I cannot believe what this boy of yours did! It was all I could do but apologize to Mother Marilyn and her daughter Mary for his conduct. I do not know what got over him! What are we going to do?" He rushed out all the words as his grip on the collar got tighter and higher, to the point that Willie was on his tip-toes.

"William, calmly tell me what's happened and for goodness sake, put the boy down. Willie come sit in this chair. I think once your father tells me what you've done, you have some explaining to do. Then we will think of a proper punishment." Once Willie was free to sit in the chair, he held his head down to hear the charges.

"He . . . He . . . He grabbed that little girl, Julia, and kissed her! In front of the whole family! She was so upset that she pushed him off and slapped him. She ran crying to her Ma, and Willie just stood there grinning like an idiot! What kind of proper behavior is that, young man? You do not kiss a girl, at your age, and NEVER without permission! That is not what a gentleman does, ever!"

"I see, William, now please calm down and close the bedroom door. We need to have a serious talk with young Willie here. Willie, come sit on the bed. William, you sit in the chair, please and breathe, your face is terribly red! I do not need you to have a heart attack over this, now do I?"

"Why are you being so calm? Did you not hear? He forced himself on Julia." Willie had not moved himself from the seat until his father shut the door and grabbed him by the collar, again, and lifted him off it. "Go sit where your mother told you, young man. Do not add to your disobedience!" Willie sat, sullenly, on the bed.

I took his hand. "Willie explain, yourself now."

He nodded and began. "I did not mean to do it. Julia's Ma was talking about her moving schools and when I asked why, Julia said that she is coming to live here with her Grandmother. The next thing I knew, I kissed her and was getting slapped! Isn't that great Mother, she is moving here?"

I looked at William, "Puppy Love. He has your big heart. You cannot blame him for being excited." Then I turned to Willie. "Young man, I know that you like Julia, but there are things that you cannot do and kissing is one of them. You will not even be seven for two more days!! You cannot kiss her again until you are Ian's age. Do you understand? Now for your punishment, I would like you to WRITE a note of apology to both Julia and her mother for your behavior and you will read it to them out loud, tomorrow after school when your father takes you to Mother Marilyn's. Now go work on that note. Think of how you hurt her feelings and overstepped the rules of society by being so bold."

Willie slipped off the bed and said, "Yes Ma-am. I will tell try."

"Willie, tell Lizzie what you want to say then copy her letters for yourself. Use your words, not hers or mine. I want to see it when you are finished." He silently left the room.

William was sitting back in the chair with his mouth open. "He likes her? He's only seven! I thought girls were icky at seven. That does explain his actions, though. You knew about this?"

"Of course, William, you only had to see the way he was around her. I knew right away! That is why Ian's news was so upsetting, I never saw the two of them together to see it coming. He kept his feelings about Lydia a secret from me and since he didn't bring her around, I had no idea. A woman can tell these things, you know."

Unbeknownst to me, Lydia was back in the doorway and heard me. "Oh, Mother Beth, I did not know that is why you were upset. I thought you did not like me." She blushes and looks down.

"Lydia, come to me, my daughter. I have always had a soft spot for you but I never knew that Ian had even talked with you. I never saw the courtship blossom. I was just caught off guard, by it all. You are smart and organized and thoughtful and are going to be the perfect wife and mother. Of this, I am sure." Lydia becomes tearful and bends down to kiss my cheek.

She walks to the doorway and turns back to me. "It is getting late, Mother, is there anything I can help you with, before Ian and I leave? I will be back tomorrow to help, too, if you don't mind."

"I would not mind it at all. Lydia, you are very sweet, and a very welcome new member to our family." With that Lydia blew me a kiss and turned and left.

Ian came back in the room for his good-bye. "Ian, would you and Lydia want to live on the property? We could build you two a small cabin. If she wants to be with family, why are you staying at the hotel? She has George, who manages it. She doesn't have to live there, does she?"

"I would like that Mother. I will talk with Lydia about it. You won't have hurt feelings if she says no, will you?"

"Of course not, she has the right to live the life she wants. It is just an idea. With the baby coming, she might want family around, anyway. Of course, I will have you back. Is it too soon to say, 'I miss you?'" I give him a wink.

"My goodness, Mother, I have been married for just two days. What if she and I went on a long honeymoon, then you can say you miss me. But two days? Good-night Mother, I will talk to my bride about it and let you know what we decide."

THIRTY-EIGHT

Saturday, October 30th, 1937
In Lawrence, Kansas

Clara Beth let Anna sleep four straight hours, last night! What a restorative thing, four hours sleep! Anna also slept well knowing that her family was finally safe! She lazily stayed in bed in Henry's arms, until eight o'clock in the morning. Hours past her usual time to start the family breakfast. She is confident that no one will be bothered by her sleeping in, today.

Yesterday, did not seem real, here in the morning's light. There were hundreds of workers on the land for the last harvest. There were all the security guards posted and her armed family members and still, John got past them all! After the Colonel saved her, the security team called the Sheriff and there were statements to be made. John's body had to be removed and the bed stripped. Carolyn threw the bedding and the mattress away. The harvest had to be finished and an evening meal had to be made. Anna could not help with any of it. The ordeal made her shake for hours afterward, even with Henry holding her.

But they got through it! The most touching moment of the night was the Colonel going to Susan and saying, "I am sorry that I had to kill your kin. He left me no choice, I hope you can forgive me." She asked him to bend down and when he did, she gave him a kiss on the cheek. "You <u>saved</u> two of my kin, tonight, Colonel. That is something to be thankful for, you and Mrs. Julia are a blessing."

Susan, then, called Mark and Melinda and told them the news. To say that they were relieved was an understatement! Melinda said that she was tired of being guarded by Mark and Petro. Of course, she loves them both for doing it, but now there is no need!

After the meal, they were just settling down when Carolyn's beau, Eddie came for the weekend and as everyone was filling him in, Anna started shaking all over again.

Eddie could hardly believe that the Colonel saved

the day. The Colonel was in the sitting room, when Eddie went and had a small chat with him. He asked him how he was doing and a few other questions. When Eddie was done, he and the Colonel rose and hugged each other. The Colonel was smiling as he sat back down and was soon fast asleep again. Eddie came back into the kitchen and said, "Wow, I cannot believe that he is the same man from before. I hope this is the new Colonel to stay!"

Anna and Henry go downstairs to the kitchen, to have their breakfast after Clara had hers. Carolyn is very excited about the party tomorrow! "Thank God, we are free to leave the Plantation. I have organized a trip to a costume shop so everyone can get an outfit for the costume birthday party! Something happy to look forward to, for a change." She was standing at the kitchen counter and Eddie had his arms around her from behind. "Tomorrow will be so much fun; I cannot wait to see Grandfather's face when he is surprised!"

She hasn't let the Colonel know that all his siblings are coming. He will be so thrilled. Her grandmother Julia, always had big parties for his birthday. The parties were the glue that held the family together, after Great-Gram Beth passed on. This will be the first one the Colonel has had since the last one Julia gave him over eleven years ago.

At ten o'clock in the morning, Henry's Da comes home in an ambulance with Dr. Mason driving. They were all very surprised that he accompanied Frank. After everyone hugged Frank and welcomed him home. The doctor explained, "Frank and I were talking about all of the events that happened here, yesterday. I wanted to make sure the Colonel, Anna and Clara were unharmed, for myself. I heard that Clara was in the room when the shots were fired. I wanted to check her hearing for any damage if she was close."

"I never thought of that," Anna said worriedly. "Clara was about ten feet away from the shotgun and only four feet from the derringer. She was screaming her head off after the shot woke her up. Do you think it was from ear pain and not just being startled?"

"How has she been after her initial crying? Is she cranky? Has she been nursing as usual? Is she responding to your voice as before?"

"Not cranky, slept very well, nursing well and I think she is responding as normal. But, now, I am worried about her. Oh, thank you for coming to check on her, Doctor."

"That is why I am here. I, also, was worried about the Colonel. For all the years in the Cavalry, I know for a fact that he never shot a man face to face, before. I wanted to see how he was holding up."

Doctor Mason did a thorough exam on the baby. He said that Anna should bring her to the Clinic next week, but all seems fine, now.

Doctor Mason then went into the sitting room and sat and talked with the Colonel for an hour or so. Finally, both men stood and shook hands. The Colonel padded off to the bathroom and the Doctor came back into the kitchen. "He is amazingly lucid. I haven't seen him this good in years. I cannot believe it. I felt that I was talking to my old friend that stood watch as his wife's health declined no matter what I tried. He took a deep decline, himself shortly after that. I do not know how long this will last, his system must still be in high alert." He looks to Carolyn and Joshua, "I expect that when he loses the adrenaline, he will regress back to the confused Colonel, we are all used to seeing.

Joshua says, "It is a shame, we never knew this Colonel. He must have been a force to be reckoned with, in his day."

"He was. Julia and my mother were good friends from childhood. The Colonel talked me into going to Med school. I was considering a military career and he said, "Better to save lives than take them." I was very moved by that and never thought about the military again.

Carolyn is surprised. "I knew you were Grandmother's doctor but I did not realize that you knew them, socially. As many years as I have known you, why have you not mentioned it?"

"I was, also, classmates with your father, Kevin. I was in Boston in Medical School when he and your mother were killed. I lost touch with your grandfather, until his Julia became ill. Your grandparents never talked about Kevin. I think it hurt them too much to remember so I never brought it up. I didn't realize that you did not know any of this. I should have, though, if he wouldn't talk about him to me, why would he talk about him to you?"

"Wow, Doctor. I am shocked by all of this. Do you think the Colonel will talk about Father, now?" Carolyn asks. "While he is still lucid, I mean?"

Dr. Mason just shrugged his shoulders. "Time heals all wounds. He might be ready. I wouldn't push him, though. Don't make it seem like an interrogation, either, and do not blame him for his silence for all these years. Grief is a very personal thing. No one can tell someone how to cope with loss."

"Of course, we will be respectful. Maybe at the costume party we can get some details. If not from him, maybe from his siblings." Joshua says. "Carolyn, speaking of the party, what time are we expected at the costume shop?"

"Oh, my goodness! In a half, an hour, we should leave! Sorry to cut you short, Doctor but we all need costumes for the Colonel's birthday party tomorrow. I know it is short notice, but did you want to come by? Costume is optional. If you knew Grandmother, did you know any of the Colonel's sisters or brothers?" Carolyn looks around and lowers her voice. "He doesn't know that they are all coming here, tomorrow. Sort of a surprise party. It is at four o'clock and we are going to party 'til the cows come home! But we all need to get out of here, now."

The Doctor hesitates. "I do remember attending your Gram Beth's funeral when I was a teenager, so I met all of the Colonel siblings, then. I felt as if I knew most of them through your father's tales of them, though. Who will stay with the Colonel and Frank? Or are they going, also? Would you like me to stay with them? And you could pick me up a costume, also?"

Carolyn is overwhelmed. "I suppose it is an understatement to say that you are a live saver! Yes, please, stay with them and we will gladly pick up an outfit for you!!"

After the shopping for costumes, everyone went back to the Main House for a large Celebration dinner. Doctor Mason stays to eat, talking nonstop with both

Frank and the still lucid Colonel.

Anna, Henry, and Frank are going to spend the night at the Little House for the first time since before Clara was born. Tomorrow is going to be a very full day. Matthew and Melinda were coming to Lawrence, in the morning. The Colonel's siblings were going to come directly to their Little House to change into their own costumes for the party, to surprise the Colonel.

They are all coming into Lawrence, despite their advanced years. None have lived here for years. Joseph, now 86, moved to Wichita for medical school and ended up setting up a small clinic there. His sister, Lizzie, now 84, went to medical school there, too. She joined him in the Wichita clinic and specialized in Gynecology and Obstetrics. Marjorie, now 73, married a man and moved to Leavenworth. Carolyn, now 72, married Julia's brother Grant and moved to EL Dorado, where he inherited a large farm from his father's father, when he turned 21. The youngest, Charles (called Chilly since childhood), 71, joined the Cavalry, just like his older brother Willie. He ended up stationed out West but settled just south of Kansas in Oklahoma, where he was a Sheriff for many years. Anna and Henry cannot wait to meet them all. They feel like they know them, from listening to Beth's Journal all month.

THIRTY-NINE

October 30th, 1866 Tuesday
An Excerpt from Elizabeth's Journal

As I am just lying in bed waiting for the babe to calm down in my womb, I realize that I have veered off the purpose of this journal. The telling of the Quantrill Massacre has taken a back seat to the events in my life. I think that is a testament to how we in Lawrence have survived.

I am happy to tell you that Quantrill and his top lieutenants have not. As I wrote here a few weeks ago, William's regiment and Senator Lane's militia as well as others were in pursuit of the raiders as they escaped into Missouri.

Many of the men who participated in the massacre, were very disappointed. They were told that Lawrence was the richest town in Kansas and that everything that they took from us would be split among the men and the good people of Missouri that hid them and fed them for months. Quantrill promised but what ended up happening is that George Todd and his crew got the bulk of the cash and kept it. None of the spoils were donated to anyone. Thinking that you are going to be a modern-day Robin Hood then see that every dime is going into the pockets of the Colonel's favorites, disenchanted many of his followers.

Many thought, that they were going up against trained soldiers and militia. What they did was gun down, terrorize, and destroy the homes and businesses of unarmed, unsuspecting innocent people. Many realized that Quantrill did not attack for the advancement of the ideals of the Confederacy, but for his own greed, glory, and fame.

The raiders that stayed with him went to Sherman, Texas to spend the fall and winter. The guerrillas acted as though they were still in Yankee territory. They took what they wanted, and from whom they wanted.

Bill Gregg was one of the first to get tired of the miscreant behavior. He went to Quantrill to get a leave of absence from him so that he could join the regular

Confederate Army. He had fought with George Todd about keeping the loot for himself and his crew and Quantrill sided with Todd. When Quantrill gave him permission to leave, he told him that his life was in danger because of his vocal displeasure of Todd.

Just before Christmas, Bloody Bill Anderson announced that he was going to get married to a local girl. Quantrill refused to grant him permission. He told him that he needs to remain focused on their War against the Unionists. Anderson pointed out that Quantrill took the time to marry Kate. They did not come to an agreement so Anderson left and took sixty-five men with him. They were the most ruthless men Quantrill had in his army.

The residents of Sherman, Texas were Confederate sympathizers but the raiders constant terrorizing of the town was making them consider becoming Yankees again. They urged the Confederate Major in charge of the area to intervene. Major McCulloch repeatedly warned Quantrill to control his men or there will be consequences.

The major problem was, Quantrill no longer had the respect, let alone, control of his men. Their behavior got so bad that a warrant for William Quantrill was issued from McCulloch's superiors. So, as a ruse, McCulloch requested a meeting with Quantrill to discuss military strategies, as they had several times. Quantrill suspected a trap. He had his men wait outside then he entered the Hotel for the meeting. McCulloch placed him under arrest and left him with two soldiers in a room while he went to have lunch. Quantrill managed to get the drop on the guards and escaped out the front door to his waiting horse.

The Raiders took off and McCulloch sent Col. J. Martin after him. As the column got closer, Bill Anderson joined in the pursuit of his former commander. The next morning, George Todd led an ambush on Martin. He warned that if they did not stop this pursuit and persecution of William Quantrill, they would kill and destroy several towns in Texas; which would make what they did in Lawrence pale in comparison. The bluff worked and Martin went back to McCulloch. He wrote his superiors that an early Spring in Missouri is the only thing that will get the Raiders out of Texas, because he has no one with brains or courage to capture Quantrill.

What McCulloch could not accomplish; time and tempers did. Todd was getting stronger and more popular with the remaining men. He challenged Quantrill multiple times and won, by not blinking first. Todd was formally elected by the men to be the new Captain. Quantrill was now a useless figurehead allowed to co-exist with Todd, if he did not dispute Todd's authority.

As April rolled around, the Raiders headed home to Missouri. The Spring of 1864 brought many of the farmers and villagers back that were evacuated by Ewing's General Order # 11. They returned to burned out homes and scorched land. When Quantrill's army of fifty made it back, there was no one that would sympathize with them or open their cupboards for them. They had already paid too dear a price for all that the Raiders had done.

Meanwhile, General Sterling Price and his 12,000 cavalrymen wanted to retake Missouri from the Yankees and sent word to all Guerrillas to keep Federal troops busy during his march up to St Louis. He sent word to Todd directly and not William Quantrill. Bloody Bill Anderson rejoined them and he and Todd wanted to attack Fayette, Missouri but Quantrill said they were too heavily armed and manned. He went with them but demoted himself to private.

The attack on Fayette turned out to be an ambush. Heavy fire came unseen from the brick courthouse in the town square. Eighteen bushwhackers were killed and forty-two wounded. More than all of Quantrill's campaigns, added together. Quantrill rode off in disgust with a dozen men, some injured. He never saw his former lieutenants again.

On October 22nd, 1864, Todd was shot in the neck by a sharpshooter near Independence, Missouri. He had begged his men for a proper burial, before dying. The men carried his body to the town cemetery and started to dig but the owner of the plot confronted them. Jessie James came forward to threatened him. If he dared to dig up his friend; they would come back and kill him and his whole family.

On October 26th, Bloody Bill Anderson was ambushed and shot twice in Richmond, Missouri. His body was staged in various ways for photos then he was beheaded. His head was mounted on a fence. An end that came too quick for the man who killed my hours-old-infant.

In December of 1864, Quantrill was en route to Kentucky in Federal Blues under the alias of Capt. Clarke to begin raiding again. He only had thirty-four men but they included Jim Younger and the James brothers, Jesse and Frank. As his activities became more notorious, a bushwhacker from Kentucky was hired to hunt him down and was given the rank of Captain, his name was Edwin Terrill. The day after Lincoln was killed (4/13/1865), Terrill engaged Quantrill and killed two men and wounded three others. Quantrill became the prey and could no longer raid.

The first week in May, Quantrill's beloved horse, Old Charley, had a loose shoe but the horse got nervous and bucked wildly at the blacksmith's and severely injured itself. As Quantrill was putting the horse down, he claimed, "This means my work is done. My career is run. Death is coming and my end is near."

A few days later on May 10th, Quantrill and his men were trapped in John Wakefield's barn. The thin walls did not stop the hail of bullets that reigned in when they refused to surrender. Some men raced to their horses and got away. Quantrill's new mount would not let him get on. He ran to another rider but was shot in the back. The bullet hit his spinal cord and paralyzed him. He fell face forward in the mud and was nearly trampled. One of Terrill's men then shot off his trigger finger as he lay helpless in the mud. Quantrill yelled, "It is useless to shoot me anymore, I am a dying man!" He gave his name as Capt. Clarke so Terrill let him stay in the Wakefield home after the Union Doctor declared the wound to be fatal.

Frank James and three men came to rescue him but he exclaimed, "Boys, it is impossible for me to recover. The war is over and I am a dying man, so let me be. Good-bye and good luck to you all."

Capt. Terrill learned that Capt. Clarke was Quantrill's alias so he came back for him. He saw that Quantrill was taken to the hospital at Louisville Prison, where he was nursed by a Priest. He converted to Catholicism and confessed his sins. He lingered in agonizing pain for weeks. He died on June 6th. He was buried in an unmarked grave in a Catholic cemetery in Louisville.

Having known the man, all those years ago, I still could not fathom why he became so cruel and greedy. I confess that I took great joy out of hearing that he suffered so, at the end. And God forgive me but I was upset that he supposedly converted to Catholicism, confessed and was forgiven his sins before he went to his maker. Then part of me knows that it was Charlie Hart's last confidence game. He was trying to pull one over on the man upstairs. Every prayer that has left my lips, since I have heard of his death include the words:

'Don't believe it for a second, Lord. Don't be fooled by him like I was!

FORTY

October 31, 1866. Wednesday
An Excerpt from Elizabeth Lewis' Journal

The morning sun was just coming up over the horizon when my pains started in earnest. I realized the date but there was nothing I could do about it. Young Willie will just have to share his birthday with the next little Lewis.

I reached over and nudged William. He just groaned his 'it's too early, don't bother me' groan. I've heard that one enough times. Whenever I wanted him to attend to one of the crying little ones, I heard it. I waited a few minutes but the pain bore down on me hard. "Uggghhh!" I cried out in anguish. "William, this is no time for snoozing! The baby is coming! You need to wake Lizzie, go get Mother Marilyn and send for Lydia. I have done nothing since the wedding except get up to use the chamber pot, but this babe wants out. He wants out today!!"

This got my large sleeping husband to open his eyes. "Beth are you sure?" He was rubbing one eye with one hand and scratching his head with the other one. He looked at me. I would have said something but another pain came on me. "Never mind. Can I get you anything before I get the others?" I could only shake my head no.

He rose and quickly dressed and went to get Lizzie. My daughter would have to miss school today. She had said that she didn't want to participate in their celebration of All Hallows Eve. She said that she has seen real Devils in person and has no interest in pretending it is something to play act about. My poor girl witnessed too much during the raid. Much too much. Another thing I blame myself for.

Lizzie came into my room, barefoot but in her robe. "Mama?" She all but whispered. "Father said, it's time? What do you need?" She went over to the bureau and took the top off the lantern, struck a match, lit the wick and replaced the glass. She came to the bed and moved the covers. "Let me check to see how far along you are." She sounded like an adult with her calm demeanor. I

184

let her peek, she held the lamp close for the inspection. "Oh, Mama, you will not have long. Have you been in pain long?"

"Maybe a little more than an hour, I guess. I was trying to ignore it. I thought he would stop this nonsense." I tried to smile for her. "I did not want to wake everyone until I was sure."

"I hope Lydia gets here fast. She might miss the whole thing. Mama, you keep calling the baby 'he', you never did that with the other babies."

"This guy is large like Ian and Willie. He has been low, the whole pregnancy. That is the way, I carried all three boys. If this is a girl, she will be harassed for her size from the start."

"If you expect a big baby, it is a good thing you are delivering early, then. I will go get water, towels and such. Joseph is going for Lydia and Father went for Grandma Marilyn. I will be back in a moment." She left the bedroom. She was right, it is a good thing that I am delivering early. Ladies, my size can be ripped apart from delivering a baby too large.

I was having another bad pain, when I heard William come back with Marilyn. Lizzie is talking with her as William comes directly to the room. "How are things, Beth? I am very worried about you. We need to make sure that you do not go through this again. This is too dangerous at your age." He grabbed my hand. "Promise me that this is the last baby, Beth. I know it is hard on you but it nearly kills me watching you go through this."

"I was going to say the same to you, William. Besides, I don't want Ian's babe calling someone younger aunt or uncle, how odd would that be? I don't have much time before this one is coming. Please do not worry, though. I will be in the experienced hands of Marilyn. Give me a kiss, before the next pain hits, and get the boys ready for school." He was holding my hand but he wasn't moving. "Go William, you do not need to see me like this. This is a woman's business. Now kiss me and go!" He did so, but left unwillingly.

Lizzie and he tried to cross the threshold of the doorway at the same time. He stepped aside and let his daughter come in. She had her hands full of linens and

185

he knew she was on a mission. He turned back as he was closing the door. He was looking at his daughter with a little smile of great pride. Then his gaze rested on me and I gave him a smile back. He gave me a wink then softly closed the door.

Lizzie was laying out all the necessary linens. I watched how calm she was moving. Of course, this was the fourth child she would help deliver. She was only ten when my doomed Clara came and Mother Marilyn and Miss. Petrie did most of the work but she was there, by my side through it all.

Mother Marilyn came in with the pot of hot water, and her little vials of medicine. Laudanum, I assume. Birthing the last two little girls, I did not get to the point of needing it but this sized babe will be so much harder to deliver. Before they are finished setting up everything that they might need, I felt another pain come down hard. "Oh, oh, oh. This is strong." Lizzie took the lantern she lit and lifted the covers again and Marilyn checked me.

"Lizzie is right, you will not have long to wait. You are almost completely dilated. I think just a few more pains and we will see the baby crowning. Is the pain still bearable? I brought Laudanum."

"I know it will make things easier but I won't remember anything of the birth, if I take that. If this is to be my last child, I want to remember it all! But what if I cannot take the pain, Mother, is there a time when it is too late?"

"No my dear, you can take it at any time. It works in just a few minutes, if you recall. I don't think you would have survived Clara's birth if _that man_ hadn't given us some." I noticed that she has never said his name. She had said once that to remember his name is to keep his fame alive, even if he is dead. Well, she wouldn't approve of my journal, then.

After three more very strong pushes, Marilyn said that she can see the baby's head coming. I called out loud, "Where is Lydia? I wanted her help through this."

"I am here, Mother Beth." She had snuck in the room and was waiting at the doorway. "What do you need?" I can hear the nervousness in her voice.

"I need my daughters at my side." I held a hand

out to her and she came rushing to kneel next to me. Lizzie was already at my other side. Another strong pain and push followed. Both the girls helped hold me up as I bared down. I felt a gush of water come out. "Oh, thank god. I was worried that my bag hadn't burst, yet."

Marilyn is positioned below me. "Beth, I am afraid that you will rip from this boy coming out. I am going to give you some Laudanum, now, and then make a nice cut that I will be able to sew up nicely when this is over. Are you okay with that?" Lizzie left my side, to get the cup of water and Mother Marilyn put just a few drops in it.

As I was feeling the effects start to wash over me. I looked at the strong women assisting me. "I am so lucky to have you all in my life. I love you all. And I love my family. Tell my William, that I love him very much, too. Will you?" I must have sounded like someone who drank a whole bottle of wine. I do not remember much after that.

I am told that my son, Charles Palmer Lewis came into this world at 11:30 am. He was the largest of all my babies. After Marilyn cleaned him, she went to hand him to Lizzie but Lizzie said, "Give my new brother to my new sister, first." I am very proud that she included Lydia that way.

Lydia then carried Charles out to meet the rest of his family. She handed him to my husband, who like his father was smiling and crying at the same time.

Or so I was told.

FORTY-ONE

Sunday, October 31st, 1937
Lawrence, Kansas

Anna woke just before dawn which is her usual time, very rested, because Clara Beth slept through the night! The baby did wake up ravenous, though. Anna was watching her sleep and saw her eyes flutter open. Her breasts were overfull from not feeding her, but Anna did not want to wake her. Clara's basket was next to the bed and she reached down, gave her a little kiss and put her straight to the breast.

Henry eased himself out of the bed and went to put coffee on. Before he left the room, he stopped and turned to look at his girls. "I need to borrow Joshua's camera. I want to show you how angelic you are when nursing our daughter."

Anna was shocked. "Don't you dare, Henry. What if Joshua see me half undressed like this, I'd be mortified. He would have to get the film developed, wouldn't he?

"I am sure that he would give me the film canister to take it in, myself." He crawled back onto the bed. "But the man who develops the film would get a good look at my beauties. I guess, I can't have that. Give us a morning kiss, my angel." She gladly kissed him tenderly. Clara, who was still nursing, reached up and broke away from the nipple and cooed at her parents. Henry looked down at her. "I am not trying to take your Mama away, my girl. I am just sharing her." With that, Clara happily gave her full attention back to her meal. Both Anna and Henry laughed.

Henry then left the room to make the coffee and check on his Da. He is worried that Frank is home too soon. Da still has a little droopiness of the face and his speech isn't back exactly like it was before. Dr. Mason did say that he should regain it with time.

They had a quick cup of coffee at home and Anna took Clara and her basket up to the Main House. Judy and Judd had breakfast started but the only other one up was Carolyn. When Anna came into the kitchen back door, Carolyn went to her. "How was being back to your Little House for the first time? You look very rested. Will it be a big bother to have my aunts and uncles use your place to change into their costumes? I knew, they would know where it is since it was my grandparents first home." Carolyn did not wait for an answer. She had the basket and was taking little Clara out and was kissing her all over. "I missed you little girl. Why do you have to live so far away?"

Judy interrupts, "Don't remind me, we'll have to go back home next week. I do not know how I will be able to be away from my little granddaughter. I do not want to think about it." She starts to get misty.

Judd puts his arms around her. "We really do not have to go, the harvests are done for the year. Matthew and I missed Grant's pumpkin and squash harvest, though he understood why we stayed here. I am not needed at the farm, right now. Matthew can handle the ordering of supplies and seeds and taking the last harvest to market for me."

"Oh, Judd, could we really stay? I cannot make myself leave my little girl, this soon." She turned and kissed her husband. "Are you sure? Won't Matthew have his hands full with school?"

Matthew and Susan come in with Eddie. "What about me and school?" He asks as he goes straight to the coffee pot and begins pouring out three coffees.

Judd explains. "Your mother and I were discussing staying on here for the winter. There are a just a few things that need to be done at the farm. I thought you could handle it, in my place."

Judy continues, "If you are too busy with school, your father can go in with you and just stay until everything at the farm is put to sleep for the winter?" She looks at Judd, they have never spent a night apart. "Judd, it would only be for a couple of days, wouldn't it?"

Before making his parents suffer living in two separate towns for even a day, Matthew would do anything they ask. "Ma, I can handle the farm business, just fine. Don't make Pa live without you for minute. He wouldn't be any good at work, without you at home, and you know it."

Judy crosses the room, makes Matthew bend down and kisses his cheek. "Such a good son. I am so blessed."

Anna looks sternly at Carolyn, "Look at what you started! Who wants what for breakfast? We have a busy day ahead! What time is Mark and Melinda coming, did they say?"

"Mark said he will be here around 11 a.m. They were going to bring Carolyn Johnson, the Colonel's sister but she is coming in with her granddaughter, Juliet. Would you believe she married Julia's big brother, Grant Johnson the first. He was our Grant Johnson's grandfather. Melinda always said, everyone was related in EL Dorado but who knew?" Matthew was laughing. "So Pa, we've been working for the Lewis family all along!"

All his Pa could say with a smile was, "Don't that beat all?"

****

It is a little after three-thirty in the afternoon and the front parlor is already very full. Everyone is in costume with a mask on. The surprise guests are all still at the Little House dressing and reacquainting with each other. Carolyn's plan was to have them come in unannounced but once they were all in the parlor, she was going to make some sort of game so that they would reveal themselves. She hasn't quite figured out what to say or do but she cannot wait to see her grandfather's face when he realizes they are all there. Joseph and Jose are going to bring the special guests in costume from the Little House before attending with their wives, themselves.

The Colonel is dressed as George Washington and he even let them put a wig on him to complete the outfit. He is a little confused today but still better than he was a few weeks ago. He tells Joshua when he is dressing him that Julia told him to kiss everyone hello from her. He did not know what that meant. Joshua almost says that Julia has a big mouth but he thought it will not do any good to start a fight with his dead Grandmother.

Carolyn and her Professor dress as Mary Todd and

Abraham Lincoln. Susan has Carolyn's hair pulled in tight ringlets like those in the photos of Lincoln's wife. Susan and Matthew have the most elaborate costumes. They are going as Marie Antoinette and King Louis of France. They also wear elaborate wigs. Matthew cannot believe that he let Susan dress him up so fancy! He really, doesn't mind. She giggles each time she looks at him and he loves to hear her giggle. Joshua is William Shakespeare, tights and all. The give-away that it is him is the cameras around his neck. He is clicking away as everyone is coming into the parlor.

Speaking of tights, Henry and Anna are going as Robin Hood and Maid Marion. Henry is not thrilled. Henry's Da is spectacular as Julius Caesar. Susan combed his hair just perfectly for the Emperor's look. Mark and Melinda are dressed as King Arthur and Queen Guinevere. The last ones to come down the stairs are Judd and Judy as Napoleon and Josephine Bonaparte. Carolyn has little name tag necklaces for everyone for their character's name, so no one needs to guess the costumes.

Promptly, at four sharp, Dr. Mason rang the front door as Teddy Roosevelt. Frank answers the door and guesses the costume correctly and says, "Well, Mr. President, you have two previous presidents here, so far. Come meet George Washington and Abe Lincoln, or would you be more impressed by Kings? We have two of those, in the front parlor." He writes 'Teddy Roosevelt' on the name tag and puts it around the neck of the Doctor. They all laugh, it is so good to have Frank and his wit back to liven things up.

A few moments later, the bell rings again and Florence Nightingale, and Cleopatra the Queen of the Nile come in. They each get their nametag necklaces and get announced by Frank/Julius Caesar. The Colonel is being entertained by Teddy and Napoleon so he doesn't notice the new guests. The next load brings the French actress Sarah Bernhardt, Queen Victoria, Henry the XVIII and Ann Boleyn. Frank cannot help himself and calls out "Another King and two Queens have joined our ranks!" There is more laughter then everyone settles back to their conversations. President Ulysses Grant rings the bell with his wife Julia Grant on his arm.

The next guest to come in is Pastor Jonas. He came as himself explaining that the only person that he'd want to be is Christ himself but he felt it was overstepping and he didn't want to make the Boss mad. Pocahontas and John Smith bring Ben Franklin with them. The last guests to arrive are Christopher Columbus and his wife.

Carolyn has the party catered. The dining room is filled with great things to pick at such as fried chicken, beef sandwiches, coleslaw, fruits, raw veggies, olives, and a variety of pickles. She hired a bartender and two waiters, who are going around asking what everyone would like to drink, but the guests are all interested in mingling, so far. Mary Todd joins Abe who is talking to King Louis and Marie Antoinette (Matthew and Susan).

The guests are sampling the food but are having some difficulty. Carolyn can tell that the masks are getting in the way of eating so she has Robin Hood and Shakespeare (Henry and Joshua) usher everyone back into the front parlor so that she can do the big reveal of everyone.

"Ladies and Gentleman, I welcome you all to the birthday party of Colonel William Clyde Lewis. George Washington, can you come up here for a moment? I would like to formally introduce you to all your guests. I am Mary Todd Lincoln also known as Carolyn Lewis." She takes off her mask. "George Washington is my grandfather and the birthday boy." He takes off his mask and the guest applaud. "I would like to introduce you to Abraham Lincoln who is Professor Edward James, and my boyfriend."

The Professor stands and removes his mask. "I would like to add, Carolyn, that I have asked your grandfather a very important question, yesterday." He approaches Carolyn then takes a knee. "You see, I am transferring to the University of Kansas in Lawrence for the Spring semester and I would like to know, Carolyn, if you would marry me?" He brings his tall hat to over his heart as he awaits her answer.

Carolyn, for a change, is at a loss for words and just nods. He stands and kisses her sweetly, in front of everyone. She throws her arms around his neck and gives him many little kisses back, as she finds her voice.

"Yes, yes, yes. Eddie, I will marry you! I love you!" She says out loud. Everyone breaks out in applause. "I am so happy, but I must continue. Oh, Shakespeare, can you take over?"

William Shakespeare stands and walks over to his sister and hugs her. He removes his mask. "I am Joshua Lewis, grandson to the Colonel." One by one he calls out the Masters foursome, Harrick trio, and the Collins Duo to remove their masks and introduce themselves. Now he is not sure how to introduce the others because he is not sure who is who. He looks around for help. "That is who we know, now when I call your character, please introduce yourself and remove your mask. Teddy Roosevelt?"

Doctor Mason stands and removes his mask. "I am Dr. Samuel Mason, friend of the family." He sits down.

"President Grant?"

He stands with his wife and says "I am Byron Brewster and this is my wife Emma." They remove their masks and sit down.

Joshua looks around, trying to make sure that the surprise guests are the last. "Christopher Columbus?" He and his wife stand. "I am Joseph Barnes and this is my wife Kate. I am foreman here at Legacy Plantation. Thank you for inviting us." They sit.

"John Smith and Pocahontas?" They both stand and remove their masks. "I am Jose Lopez and this is my wife Juanita. We are lucky to work for the Lewis family, also."

Joshua and Carolyn confer with each other for a few seconds. They are not sure who to call on next. They know they are all siblings of the Colonels but do not know which one is which. Joshua thinks of something. He says to Carolyn, "I've got this."

They turn back to the guests. "All those that have not revealed yourself, will you come to the front, please." They are slow to rise but do so. He whispers to them. "Can you stand in birth order please?" He says so that the Colonel cannot hear from the couch. They rearrange themselves and Joshua says, "Thank you, that makes it easier. Ben Franklin please introduce yourself."

"I am Joseph Lewis, oldest sibling to William." The

Colonel is on his feet. Tears in his eyes.

Florence Nightingale immediately goes next. "I am Lizzie Lewis, oldest sister to William. She removes her mask and tears are already falling as she sees her brother.

Cleopatra goes next. "I am Marjorie Long, the next sibling after William." She removes her mask.

Queen Victoria removes her mask. "I am Carolyn Johnson, the youngest sister to William. I love you, big brother."

Henry the XVII says, "I am Charles Palmer Lewis, called Chilly by my siblings. I am baby brother to them all and this is my wife, Brenda." Ann Boleyn and her King Henry take off their masks.

That is all the siblings but there is one person left. Joshua asks, "Sarah Bernhardt, who are you?"

She removes her mask and her simple beauty takes Joshua's breath away. She sees Joshua's reaction and blushes three shades of red. She says just barely above a whisper, "I am Juliet Helen Johnson. I am Carolyn Johnson's Great-granddaughter."

Joshua is just staring at her. His sister Carolyn says, "Welcome to Legacy Plantation, everyone. Happy birthday to you Grandfather and Uncle Charles!"

Charles is surprised that she knew that. "Who told you it was my birthday, also? I told all my siblings that I did not want to take from Willie's day." He looked around to see if he could see the guilty party.

"If you want someone to blame, you'll have to talk to your mother." He looks at her is surprise. "We just read about your birth in Beth's Journals. We found almost forty of them upstairs in an old trunk and we have been reading them every night on the anniversary of the passage."

Carolyn talks to the guests again. "Grandfather, I know that you want to get reacquainted with your siblings but I wanted to invite just one more guest." She walks over to the parlor's entryway where the Sampler hung that was found in the trunk. On the table under the hung sampler was Beth's first Journal. She opened it up. "We found this sampler and many of these books last month, written by Beth Lewis. I would like to read a small excerpt from it, as a way of bringing Gram Beth to the Party."

November 1ˢᵗ, 1866. Thursday
An excerpt from Elizabeth Lewis's Journal.

I decided to stitch a Sampler to hang in the front parlor. It will simply read 'The Lewis Legacy'. I will stitch an identical one for each of my children, also. My Sampler, will have individual miniatures hanging from it with the name of each of my children so that they all will know that they are a part of a great unfinished story that we each create day by day. On their Sampler, I will only stitch their own name, but eventually their spouses and children can have their own names hanging, too. This way they will know that what they will bring to our story and to future generations is their own Lewis Legacy.

Carolyn looks around at her guests, her new fiancé and all her family, and smiles. "Let's eat, shall we, there is a ton of food in the dining room and I for one, am starving. Pastor Jonas, will you say Grace before we dine?"

"For this family, Carolyn, it would be my honor."

THE END

ABOUT THE AUTHOR

Cherisse M Havlicek writes from her home in the beautiful town of Bridgman, Michigan. She has been married for over thirty years to a now retired Chicago Police Officer. Raised in the suburbs of Chicago, she fell in love and married him in 1985 and when he retired from the Police Force in 1999, they had a seven-year-old boy, Arthur, and a two-year-old girl, Alisse. They knew that they wanted to live in Michigan, where they had been coming up on weekends for decades! Cherisse has a varied work experience. She was a Hairdresser, an interior landscape horticulturist, a clerk at Cook County Juvenile Court, and in Michigan she worked at a daily Newspaper where she went from a Route manager to Single Copy manager to the top producer in the Advertising Dept. while raising her children, and attending their sports activities. She also helped take care of her husband's elderly mother and his disabled cousin, that lived with them, at the time.

As they became 'empty nesters', her husband was diagnosed with Lewy Body Dementia with Parkinson's. She knew that she could no longer work full time out side of the home. She was a wholesale rep for a time then sold antiques at a local store but even that took her away from home too much.

In September of 2016, her grown son, Arthur, found chapter one of a book she started in high school and gave her grief about not finishing it. She wrote the next forty-five chapters in eight months and her first novel *ANNA AT LAST* was complete. She didn't stop there, though. She wrote *THE LEWIS LEGACY* while her husband had his back surgery and during his rehab. Then last installment in the A Present / Past Saga series - *JUSTICE FOR JOSHUA* was also written in 2018. She has also written a Children's Christmas story called *A SILENT NIGHT.* These works will soon be available for purchase. She, obviously, is making up for lost time and has no plans to stop.

You can connect with her on her Facebook page:
Author – Cherisse M Havlicek

Made in the USA
Monee, IL
25 August 2022

11694519R00121